I0781140

THE KALEIDOSCOPE

A.P. ROYAL

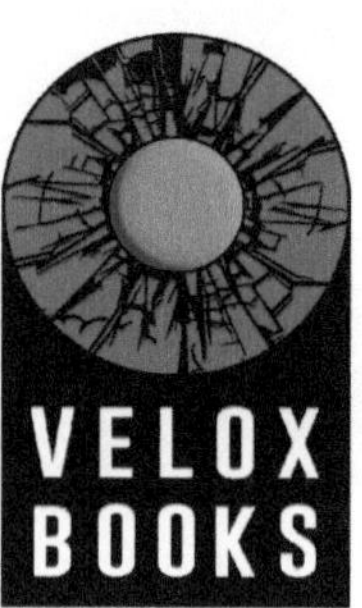

Published by arrangement with the author.

Copyright © 2025 by A.P. Royal.

All rights reserved.

No part of this publication may be reproduced, distributed, or transmitted in any form or by any means, including photocopying, recording, or other electronic or mechanical methods, without the prior written permission of the publisher, except as permitted by U.S. copyright law.

The story, all names, characters, and incidents portrayed in this production are fictitious. No identification with actual persons (living or deceased), places, buildings, and products is intended or should be inferred.

YOU'RE READING ANOTHER TERRIFYING COLLECTION FROM

**FOLLOW VELOX TO KEEP
THE NIGHTMARES COMING:**

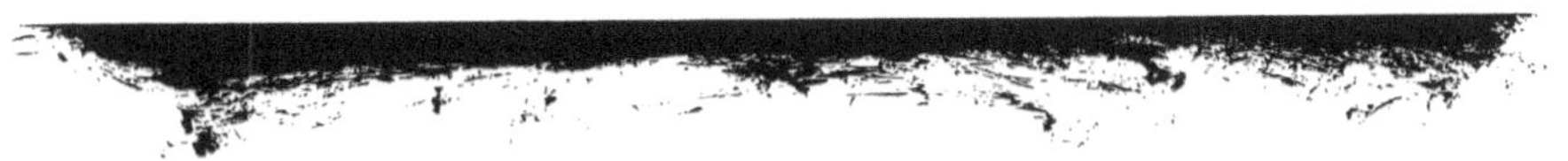

Thanks & Love:

To my wife, Cristina: Thank you for your overwhelming love and support over the years in everything and anything that I do. Our success is always a product of your sacrifices.

To my daughters, Livy & Fiora: I hope you find what you love and chase it.

To Mom and Dad: Thanks for fostering a love of reading in me from an early age.

To John G.: You gave me that little push when I needed it the most. This book doesn't exist without you.

To the NoSleep community: You are amazing and will always hold a dear place in my heart.

And lastly, Velox Books: Thank you for making all of this work mean something.

Visit A.P. Royal online:
www.aproyal.com

CONTENTS

THE GULLY

Wyatt Flemming went missing in the summer of '19.

There was no write-up in the newspaper, no six o'clock special on the evening news.

To his loved ones, he was lost a long, long time ago, when he chose life on the streets over the recovery center. To the city, it was easier if someone like him disappeared. Council overwhelmingly supported the relocation bill. Their policies had the goal of revitalizing the streets of Freemont resulting in a safer downtown core. All the tents were folded up, the shopping carts loaded into vans. Hundreds of vagrants and streetwalkers were displaced from the corners and alleyways that they had occupied for years. They were shipped from the bustling downtown metropolitan area to the outskirts of the city limits, near the forests and the gravel trails that led to the Gully. Far away from the five-star restaurants, the high rises, and the boutiques, they were dumped near the newly erected rehab facilities and low-income housing projects.

As far as the city was concerned, they had all disappeared.

So, no one batted an eye, no, not for a vagrant. If he wasn't my brother, I probably wouldn't have cared either.

During my weekly wellness check—a piping hot styrofoam plate filled with a serving of meatloaf in hand—I took the typical route along the tree line, just off the gravel path. When the scent slapped you—the razor-sharp whiff of acidity, of piss—you knew you were heading in the right direction.

I slowly trotted down the embankment to his usual spot. The blue, tattered polyethylene tarp hung across four pencil-thin pines. His pile of clothes underneath reeked of whiskey and unwashed armpits. It was a saddening excuse for a dwelling, but to Wyatt, it was home.

As you got closer, the smell worsened. The scent choked you, forcing a palm to the bridge of your nose. A rusty shopping cart with the Pay-Less logo on the handle was pushed up against a fallen tree, filled to the brim with a man's life-long accumulation of possessions. Nestled into the carefully curated blanket of leaves and foliage pillows, his el-natural mattress, lay a lonely, half-empty bottle of Jack.

That's when I knew something was wrong. Those two were inseparable.

I trudged through the rows upon rows of trees, ignoring the pricks from the pine-needle arms that brushed up against you, pulling you in. I followed a squishy dirt-moss-leaf soup, a thin trail of murky water that seemed to lead deep into the forest.

I called out for Wyatt, hoping the trees would carry my voice to him.

I checked for footprints or signs of struggle, anything that would lead me to my brother. The search lasted hours before I realized I was at the edge of the forest, footsteps from the entrance of the Gully. There was nowhere else to go.

It was a steep drop-off; the side of the hill had caved in to form a deep ditch. Inside the ditch was a dark pool. As kids, we used to call it the "Witch's Cauldron". The murky water was an indication that a storm was brewing. The belly of the Gully—full.

I called out for Wyatt, again and again. His name echoed across the forest with no answer.

I returned to his home every couple of days for the next two weeks, hoping to spot my brother. The bottle of Jack was still in bed, all alone.

Feeling anxious for his wellbeing, I contacted anyone of relevance that I could think of: the police, the Freemont Herald, the Channel Five News. Anyone that would listen.

No one batted an eye, no, not for a vagrant.

The expansive stretch of forest was divided in two by the rip in the earth that we called the Gully. To the north were popular hiking trails and picnic spots for the family. To the south is where Wyatt lived, near the relocation housing effort. The police reported that they had searched the entire south side looking for my brother. They searched the adjacent river, the one that fed spring water from the mountains to the city for consumption. They told me it was highly unlikely he had made it to the other side given the depth of the Gully and even more unlikely that the Gully had been full. It would have taken a torrential downpour to cascade enough water from the river into the carved bowl. Their best guess was that he fell down the cliff and tumbled into the river where his body was carried somewhere downstream. How far downstream? They weren't sure.

Their solution was a four-by-four yellow sign at the entrance of the gravel trail that read: PLEASE KEEP OUT OF THE GULLY.

The legacy of my brother was reduced to an image of a stick person, falling. A metal pole stuck in the ground was all that was left.

I punched the hood of my car as I left the precinct. "Fuck 'em," I muttered to myself. "If they can't find answers, then I will."

"This city's gone to shit," my friend Cole declared in the backseat of my car. He had his head poking out of the window, his long, stringy strands flopping in the wind. Outside of the city limits, we passed pumpjack after pumpjack on our way to the Gully.

"What are you complaining about, Cole?" my other friend, Shariff, scoffed. "How else do you plan on paying for that big-ass apartment?" He looked back at him, "Nobody eats in a recession."

Cole rolled up the window. The flashlights rolled around in the backseat. "I just mean it used to be better. Before the bloody foreigners went and bought up all the real estate."

He wasn't wrong. Business was booming in the city as we rode another economic peak, awaiting the valley, and the inevitable crash that was destined to follow. It was the rollercoaster ride of the oil and gas sector. You had no choice but to hold on and hope you survived the ride.

The transient community wasn't the only one being forced out of Freemont. The city had become popular. It had a lot to offer: low taxes and close proximity to the mountains. Things were changing quickly; you could feel it. New property development was popping up everywhere you turned. Apartment units were being stacked to the sky, one on top of the other. Developers were snapping together these lego-piece homes as high and as wide as the city permitted. To find anything affordable, you had to look else-where. The average person was pushed further and further toward the outskirts, resulting in urban sprawl.

A lot of the city's essential services quickly followed suit—the recycling facilities, the water treatment plants, the dump—they all had to be relocated further and further away as the city expanded.

I parked the car, and we walked past Wyatt's memorial sign. The wind bit through my fleece jacket, an odd chill for a summer evening.

Everything in his home was how he left it—the piss stench, the half-empty bottle.

We continued south, hollering his name, flicking on our flashlights as the sun began to dim. We passed other homeless encampments, other campers finding solace in the wilderness. Those that were coherent had confirmed they hadn't seen Wyatt in a while.

"We need to cover way more ground," Shariff said. "I think we should split up. It will be dark before you know it."

We agreed to meet back at the sign at 9:30pm, marching off in our separate directions.

I turned over logs and peeked under bushes, yelling his name all the while. There were still no signs of him anywhere. No passed-out body, no trace of footsteps.

When 9:30pm hit, and the sun began to hide behind the huddle of trees, I made my way back to Wyatt's encampment. The sky was charcoal grey, the rain pattering down soft droplets that were partially sheltered by the canopy of the trees.

En route, I heard a howl so deafening it rustled the trees. It made my stomach turn as I sped off in the direction of the sound.

"Wyatt!"

I sprinted toward the screaming, the trees scratching and clawing at me as I ducked and weaved through. It led me to the edge of everything. I stared down into the Gully. Smoky-black water sloshed around the rocky barrier, tree branches and floating debris trapped inside the carved-out crevice. No sign of Wyatt. Just murky-grey puddles around the edge of the cliff. A thin trail of it coming from the forest.

"Wyatt!"

I followed the trail of slosh to a dead end in the middle of the forest. The abrupt stop gave me goosebumps, tingling up my spine.

It was pitch-black now, water pouring down from a dense arch of clouds above. Every rustle, every stir, made me wield the beam of light in my hand like a sword. I heard long, drawn-out moans that made me shudder. I tried to trace my steps back through the void, the never-ending maze of trees. It felt like I was making loops upon loops, the trees' sharp fingers pointing me around in circles.

I had never been so happy to smell the odor of urine. I had no idea how long I had been out there before the piss-tent revealed itself.

Just past the blue tarp, I could make out a figure. Another beam of light. "Shariff? Cole?"

I shone the light on the figure's chest. His long, stringy hair was drenched and covered in leaves. "Cole! Where's Shariff?"

His eyes widened. His stare was empty and astray.

"I was hoping he was with you..."

When Payton Mckenzie disappeared, the public finally began to take notice. Pictures of her were popping up everywhere: her shiny, gilded locks curled up into spirals, her sky-blue eyes staring back at you with a glimmer of optimism that only children have. She had a face that people cared about. It was the face of innocence.

A cropped photo of her in what looked like a family portrait was plastered on every light pole and mailbox in suburbia. The flyer read: *Payton Mckenzie—Help bring her home*. The story spread like wildfire. Every news outlet played the same fifteen-minute interview with her parents. Her mom and dad begged the public for help, red rims around their eyes. *We won't stop until we find her.*

Their extended family was enjoying a picnic get-together on the north side when it happened. Payton's parents lost sight of her, only for a moment, caught up in the casual mingling around the barbecue. She must have wandered off, just a little too far from her other siblings and cousins. And a little too close to the Gully.

After Shariff's disappearance, the local police had me under a microscope. I had nothing to hide, so I told them everything. The cops completed another search with the canine unit sniffing out the trails, divers searching the river, and rescue boats looking for bodies. They all came back with nothing.

But someone like Payton didn't just go missing. Not without public outcry.

The story broke the hearts of every mother and father in the city. Search parties were organized and candlelight vigils were scheduled immediately. We needed to bring the girl home, the one that could have easily been our daughter. We had all enjoyed picnics north of the Gully at one time or another. We had all hiked a trail in that neck of the woods before.

I decided to join the search party because I needed something to do, anything to fill the sunken emptiness that festered in the pit of my stomach. I considered the blood of Shariff to be on my hands. And while part of me feared the worst, I still had to believe he and my brother were still out there.

***

There must have been fifty of us gathered in the north side parking lot. We were equipped with flashlights in hand and whistles around our necks. I was placed in a group with Paul—a lanky fellow with a crooked grin—and an older lady named Edith who came bundled up in a cardigan.

Payton's mom, Gweny, held up a map that had been sectioned off with colored markers. She motioned to our group with a gentle smile that did not match her bloodshot eyes, "You guys search the southwest corner—here."

She pointed to the map. The southwest corner: the pocket of land closest to the Gully.

This side of the Gully was much less wild. The trees seemed to crowd you less, their stalking felt much less forceful. It made you feel like you could actually breathe, like today, maybe just maybe, we had a fighting chance at finding answers.

The north side had gone through extensive landscaping to create a family-friendly picnic destination. It was a park initiative that council felt made the city more attractive. It had worked; typically, the barbecue pits were booked up solid for the summer. That was all before Payton's disappearance.

Scattered screams for Payton traveled through the forest. Groups of us headed in opposite directions on our dead girl scavenger hunt.

We searched for a couple of hours, hiking the woods, examining smudges in the dirt that could have been footprints. Everyone playing detective.

Eventually, we stopped for a break. The unstable terrain and occasional incline had knocked the wind out of Edith.

"I just need a moment," she said, beads of sweat collecting on her forehead. She leaned against one of the trees. "You young'ins don't know what it's like to have seventy-year-old knees."

Paul and I chuckled. The afternoon sun looked like it was baking every bit of his pasty skin. His face was beet-red, sweat dripping down his smooth forehead. He pulled out a granola bar and chewed as we all waited in silence.

It started with a trickle. A thin trail of earthy-grey. The liquid snaked around a cluster of trees, in a slow drizzle. I wouldn't have even noticed it had we not come to a complete stop. I watched it pool up slowly. The murky grey getting darker and more opaque. Paul and Edith were staring off into space, observing the tops of the trees. Payton's name was echoing in the distance.

I didn't think much of it at first. It could have been a tiny leak from a nearby drainpipe or maybe some sort of tiny offshoot from the river. But the puddle got deeper. Too deep—spreading out in a small wave behind a tree.

"Uh... guys?" I shouted.

The shallow puddle had gathered into a thick, sludgy pool that had oozed itself around Paul's feet. Before he could look down, a mucky tentacle wrapped itself around him. It yanked him under, the pool swallowing him up. His body disappeared into the viscous glob like quicksand. He let out an ear-splitting scream.

"Oh my God!" Edith shrieked.

I tried to lunge at him, hoping to grab an arm and pull him out. Its orange beady eyes glared back at me.

And then they were gone.

I rushed after it. Edith, with her geriatric knees, slowly followed behind. My legs were wobbly, and my heart thrashed in my chest. The thing that consumed Paul was steadily flowing away.

The thick gob was almost swimming now, moving like a viscous tidal wave, weaving in and out of the trees in the trail of liquid it had entered in. It left behind a sticky residue that blended in with the dirt. Items were being displaced from the monster, slipping out of the gob's core in a slimy film:

A mixed-berry crumble wrapper. Tiny shoe laces. A styrofoam plate.

It was leaving behind a strong smell in the wet left-behinds. A mix of methanol and grease and the rotting stink of decay.

I chased with all my might, chasing this thing that was now moving like it was sliding down a slip-and-slide at the local water-park.

I could see it now: the frac chemicals, the garbage, the human intestines. All swirled up in a big old pot. All brewing for years in the Witch's Cauldron.

My lungs burned as I watched the thing wash away down the side of the eroded cliff. Into the Gully. I peered down, in horror, as the thing slid into the belly. The dark pool swished around in the eroded half-pipe. Its nightmarish orange eyes blinked back at me.

Edith caught up to me a few minutes later, gasping for air. Others followed after hearing all of the commotion. We looked on, helplessly, but the orange eyes had disappeared into the swirling liquid.

Payton's search party came up empty. The police's search of the north side came up empty.

All they had were our stories: first-hand accounts of a monster from Edith and myself. A senile lady and a whack job obsessed with a hole in the ground, those were the labels that they gave us.

In the fall of '19, they took a man into custody named Alphonso Heraldo. He was a low-life rapist and career criminal. They said that he had been camping out in the Gully and preying on random victims. They said they had his DNA, but I never heard about any recovered bodies. He had a receding hairline and piercings coupled with raven-black eyes.

He had a face that people despised. It was the face of guilt.

It wasn't the fairytale ending for Payton Mckenzie, but at least it was an ending.

A few weeks after the unsuccessful searches, I tried to stop by the Gully to visit Wyatt's home. I noticed the sign had been replaced. Tall barbed-wire fences and plastic boards now covered the area. Miles of chainlink now confined the vast forest. Hundreds of advertisements hung from the metal fence poles, showcasing new coffee shops and restaurants opening up in the city. The signs change, but the fences still remain.

I haven't slept much since that final visit. In my nightmares, I feel a layer of oily muck sliding up my face. Its slimy tentacles wrap around me in a vice-grip, restricting my movement. I try to scream, but I drown in the sludge.

In this up-and-coming city, we have pushed away a dark secret. For years.

I noticed something this morning when I was making my coffee. I was reading the paper, patiently waiting for my bread to toast. As I took a sip of water, the way the light hit the glass, I could make out a faint hue. A pale tint of ashy-grey.

I ran to the sink and spat out the water.

This city *has* gone to shit.

WOUNDED

Mallory was late. It was nearly two hours past their court-ordered pickup time. Josie and Ally were getting antsy, their stuffed teddies in hand and backpacks stuffed to the brim.

"Did Momma forget?"

"No, Ally," I lied. "She's just running a bit late. Hang tight."

With their bedtime quickly approaching, we putzed around the foyer while I pondered what to do. Six phone calls went straight to voicemail. I sighed heavily, my mind jumping to the most devastating but logical conclusion.

So, I decided. She didn't leave me any other options.

"Okay, kids. I've got a surprise."

There was a temporary glimmer in their bored, glazed-over eyes.

"Surprise sleepover with Nanny!"

Ally grinned, letting out a cheer.

Josie rolled her eyes. Under her breath, she whispered, "I guess she really did forget..."

After a quick phone call to Grandma, the kids were sent upstairs to change into their pajamas and unpack their things. Grandma dropped everything and was over in less than twenty minutes. I graciously hugged her goodbye, leaving some money on the counter for late-night snacks.

"Leon," she called out as I slipped on my jacket.

"Yes, Mom?"

"Be careful."

The highway did its best to soothe the tumultuous swirl of thoughts in my mind. The roads were peaceful, the radio turned off. Streetlight after streetlight. Exit after exit. I tried my best to clear my head, to remain calm. It was difficult because late-night driving had always been a time for reflection, and the ghosts from the past kept resurfacing.

It was an honest mistake.

It's fine.

She's just forgotten.

I paid the toll and passed through the turnpike; all the while, the lump in my throat never settled.

This was *her* week. She never missed her week without some kind of notice. Especially considering how hard she had battled for custody and all the progress she had made; there was no way in hell she would jeopardize everything.

The gate to Scenic Acres was wide open. It was rusted and weathered—well past its time, like many of its residents. It was a quiet community, which was exactly why Mallory had chosen it: fewer opportunities to get into trouble and fewer reasons to be out late. All the houses looked the same in the twilight: cedar-shake rooftops and bungalow-style homes with faded vinyl siding in soft grey and blue tones.

The car came to a crawl as I poked my head out of the window. I squinted to see the house numbers:

#501... #503... #505.

Once I turned the corner towards Mallory's place, I noticed the lights were off on #515. The street along the block was lined with cars. I parked down the road and walked toward her home, my heart fluttering all the way to the door. The doorbell rang. I waited another moment before ringing it again, knocking a few more times for good measure.

"*Mallory?*"

No response. I drifted towards the side of the house and peered into the window. One of the plants looked like it hadn't been watered in weeks. And was that a chair toppled over?

The scene inside the house triggered flashbacks: her body on the floor in a puddle of vomit, shallow breathing before she faded out. Her stare was seared into my memory forever—the emptiness within her eyes, completely vacant of life. And I could do nothing but cry. She was gone.

Somehow the paramedics pulled off a miracle. They shocked the life back into her, pulling her from a place unknown. Those seconds had felt like decades, whimpering in a heap beside her unconscious body.

I vowed I would never let that happen again.

I ran for the back gate. Standing on my tippy toes, I dangled my hands over the top. I fished for the carabiner, eventually fumbling it open with a satisfying click. The door swung open to reveal a jungle of tall grass. The wild blades swayed in a strange wave, riding the gust of wind.

I shut the door to the backyard and hollered her name. Shorts had been a poor choice for the evening. The grass was sticky and a cloud of mosquitos hovered around my body, latching onto any bit of exposed skin. I felt a pinch on my calf and swatted my leg in a feeble attempt to scare them away.

"*Mallory?*"

I cleared the corner, catching a glimpse of the faint glow coming from the basement. Stumbling up the back porch in a panicked haste, I tried my luck with the doorbell again. I knocked aggressively, the thuds echoing into the night, but there was still no answer. Just as I prepared to send my elbow through one of the windows, the door creaked open.

The darkness was endless beyond the door; I could barely make out the figure. If it wasn't for his bleach-dyed hair he would have blended in with the sea of shadows.

"What do you want?" the voice asked.

"Where the fuck is Mallory, Chase? Is she okay?"

"She's fine, Leon. We're busy right now, though. I'll have her give you a call later tonight." Before he could close the door, I wedged my arm into the gap.

"She missed pickup, Chase. Her week was supposed to start today."

"Ahh, no. Really?" he said with feigned sadness. "Shit. I'm really sorry."

"You sure she's alright? This schedule isn't new. I had the kids all ready to go and everything, you should have seen their faces."

He pushed, but I managed to wrestle the door open. The droopy figure of Chase stood there, stupidly. Helpless and out of breath. He looked like a toothpick, his bare chest sunken, his baggy cargo shorts barely hanging on to his bony hips. But it was his eyes that were most disturbing—they were a milky pink, like two partially sucked gumballs.

"For God's sake, Chase. I knew it. You two are using again!" I stormed down the hall and into the darkness. "You're nothing but a goddamn junkie. I knew it. I'm not letting you drag her down with you. Mallory? Where are you?"

"Get out of our house," Chase ordered. I suddenly felt a hand claw at my neck in the dark. It felt clammy as I shrugged it off. As my eyes adjusted, I felt around the wall for a light switch. Before I could find it, I spotted the dull puddle of light creeping in from underneath the basement door.

"*Our* house?" I scoffed back, leaving him in the dark. "I paid for the friggin' thing."

"Leon, leave!" Chase pleaded. But I was already down the stairs.

An odd funnel of air hit me. With every creaking step, it got progressively warmer. The air seemed to cling to my body like a layer of honey, carrying with it a gurgling stench of wet laundry. A sickly hissing could be heard from the dying furnace off in the distance. I could make out the source of the light now: numerous candles were laid across the floor with no discernable pattern. Piercing red orbs of light were in every corner of the room. The heat lamps radiated waves of sweltering heat that made the walls sweat. When I finally got to the bottom of the stairwell, she was lying there, face up.

"Mallory!" I cried.

She was stiff and unresponsive, her eyes rolled back into her skull. The floor was no longer concrete like I had remembered; she laid on an earthy layer of sediment that was soft and squishy. The moisture from the soil felt wet on my bare knees as I crouched over Mallory's body. I felt for a pulse, shocked by the scene that I had prayed I would never relive.

She wasn't the only one. There were other bodies spread out haphazardly on the dirt.

"Do not touch her," a voice commanded. "You are disrupting the process."

"What did you do to her?" I screamed. "What did you do to... to... *all of them*?"

I noticed before he could answer. The dark bruises on Mallory's body were like pools of oil. They were dark islands along her alabaster-white skin. The inky blotches ran up her thigh and spread across her abdomen. Rage began to erupt inside of me.

"*Me?*" Chase mocked. "I did nothing. Nothing at all. *They*, however, are doing her a service. Quite frankly, it's *them* you should be thanking. They are doing what you could never do." He pointed in Mallory's direction.

"You son of a bitch," I growled.

"Just look."

I didn't see them at first; the fury had blurred my concentration. All I could think about was putting my fist through Chase's face. I would wring his little neck out when all of this was over, and if she didn't make it, then God help him, my rage would have no end. Mallory was still unresponsive. When I lifted her head up, gently cradling it under my arm, only then did I see them start to sway. It was the same ripple effect that could be seen on a hot summer day: the sun's rays refracting off the pavement in a strange, wavy illusion. Their movement was the only thing that made them visible, it caused a distortion between the dim glow of the candlelight that washed over the basement. If you blinked too quickly you could almost miss it. Tiny angel-hair thin strings of translucent fibers were undulating back and forth like tall blades of grass in the wind. They were sprouting up from tiny pores in Mallory's skin, wriggling around in a hypnotic dance before dipping in and out of her like an animal at a watering hole. I couldn't tell whether they were coming or going, only that they were crawling all over her body.

Vomit threatened to jump from my throat as a group of them wiggled out of her eyes. I choked the reflex away but it teetered on the brink of resurfacing.

A new sound had bolted out of me. It was akin to a yelp from a tiny dog. It escaped from my quivering lips and was met with a high-pitched hiss from Mallory's body.

"See what you've done now? You've angered *them*."

Chase crept alongside her body as I found myself drifting further and further away. I could hear the little boy inside of me, urging me to run.

"What the fuck, Chase?"

"You fool."

There was a knocking coming from the walls that I couldn't pinpoint in the shadows.

Chase wrapped an elastic band around Mallory's arm and jabbed her with a syringe. The contents slowly drained out of the needle. The hissing intensified as the ripples became stronger. I saw the little hairs on their bodies as my eyes adjusted to their camouflaged figure. They dived inside of her. In and out. Sucking and sucking, waving their thin frames from side to side in a temporary, triumphant jiggle before proceeding to feed again. I noticed that the bruises seemed to be moving, drifting, ever so slightly.

"*Feast*," Chase encouraged in a breathy whisper. "Take it all away—the chemicals, the toxins, the dependency. Take it!" He laid down beside Mallory and strapped himself up before sinking a needle into his own arm.

Another frenzy of loud knocks sent my gaze upwards. From the basement window above, I could see them pounding desperately to get in. They were much more visible given the sheer numbers of them crowding the window. Their bodies were clear like jellyfish, their mouths twisting and turning, their tiny teeth spread out and swirling like the head of a beautiful flower. Long, puffy tubes of flesh that looked as big as your hand.

It was enough to send me scampering up the stairs. Working off memory, I felt around the pitch-black room. A picture frame tumbled to the floor, the glass shattering on impact. I felt an electric shock of pain as my hip collided with the bench in the foyer. It felt like an eternity before I finally found the knob to the front door. Once free from the house, I did not breathe until I was back in my vehicle.

It was a long ride home.

Mallory called me a couple of hours later. She apologized profusely, reassuring me that everything was okay and that she was trying something new that seemed to be working. She promised to make it up to me and the kids. I let her talk. There were a lot of promises made, a lot of promises that I hoped she could keep.

When she arrived the following morning, she looked amazing. Her hair looked fuller, her smile radiant. The bags under her eyes seemed to be gone, but the bruising was impossible to hide. There was a speckle of dark purple around her collarbone, sitting above the neckline of her cardigan.

"I know. It's a little... out of the box, Leon. But I'm telling you, it's been working, like nothing else I've tried before. That gnawing feeling, you know, that urge that picks away at you... it's completely gone. It's been amazing! I finally feel free."

"*Out of the box,*" I scoffed. "Did he tell you that he shot you up while you were passed out? I thought you were *clean*, Mallory. Hell, at one point, I thought you were dead. It's not okay."

The kids were packing their bags upstairs, their excited voices travelling down to the foyer. Chase was waiting in the car outside.

"That's part of it... for now. At least until we build up enough clientele and have a large enough stable."

I shot a puzzled look in her direction. "What the fuck are you talking about, Mallory?"

"A stable, you know. I guess you could call it our new business venture," she smiled. "We already have a handful of clients, those people that you saw yesterday. You know, it's not too late to invest. We could really use the capital." She stopped by the front window and flashed an open palm to Chase, indicating five more minutes. He looked unimpressed. "Anyways, Chase thinks it could get really big. We're looking into the potential market. Hopefully we can sell the bigger ones once they mature. Eventually, they become too big for the detox process and become useless. We've just been housing them in the backyard until they eventually die. Bug farming is the next big thing, Leon. It's going to make big waves in the protein market."

I couldn't believe what I was hearing. At a loss for words, I shook my head.

She leaned in and hugged me tightly. I suddenly felt warm. "Thanks again for checking in on me last night."

There was playful cooing coming from the top of the stairs followed by frantic footsteps as the girls raced down.

"Grab your things and head to the car," Mallory ordered. They hugged me goodbye and ran to the vehicle.

"What exactly were those things, anyway?" I asked. Peering out the front window, I saw Ally showing Chase her brand-new keyboard.

"To be honest, Leon, I don't really know. Chase thinks they're part of the mealworm family. Some of them must have traveled back with me; you remember my Ayahuasca retreat a couple of months ago?"

I nodded. The much-anticipated trip to Costa Rica. "But they're safe, right?"

"They're harmless."

"And you're sure?"

"About as deadly as an earthworm. We've been working with them for a while now, Leon."

I sighed. "Just promise me you'll keep them away from the bugs, Mallory? I'm dead serious."

"Of course, of course," she smiled.

Before she left, she gently clutched my arm. "Thanks again. Seriously," she winked. "I'll bring them back bright and early for you. Have a good week." She closed the door behind her and ran into our daughter's outstretched arms in a playful embrace. I felt myself tremble as I watched their vehicle leave the driveway.

She left before I could tell her.

I wanted to tell her that my calf had swelled up last night. I wanted to tell her that the bruise had seemingly traveled to my thigh, overnight.

I wanted to tell her so many things.

THE CRANE GAME

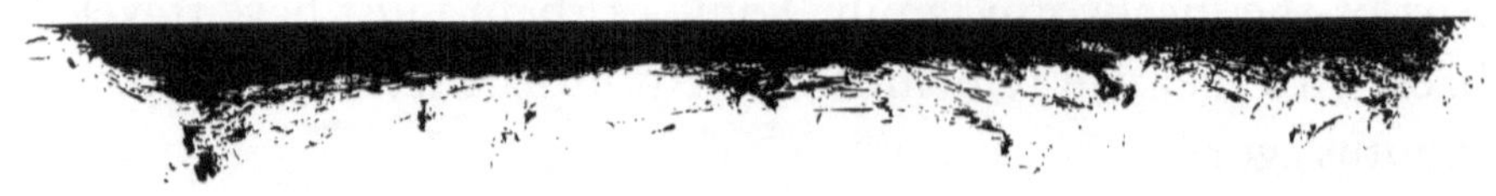

Before the pit, I was a dancer. A triathlete. A cancer survivor. I was many things, *before*. Now, I wasn't sure what was left of my prior self. One thing was for certain: I was a prisoner. Held against my free will. Unsure if I had the will, or the luck, to make it out of that place alive.

I woke up, face down, in a puddle of drool, saliva leaking from the corner of my mouth. I was unable to see past the dusty floor, unable to move or cry for help. No matter how hard I focused or how hard I tried, it was like the synapses in my brain were misfiring to the rest of my body.

So, I laid there and listened to the music—the trumpets and tubas in a rapid tempo—playing from the speakers somewhere, everywhere, around us.

I couldn't see them, but I could hear them. Their listless cries for help. Their screaming, their moaning, their heavy, helpless screams overtop of the repetitive tune. They would eventually tire, leaving the tune to fill the silence once again.

The melody, on repeat, triggered memories of my father and the carnivals he used to take me to as a child. He would lead me past the rows of food stands, our hands together, intertwined. Smells of popcorn, cotton candy, and deep-fried atrocities filled the air. The rides looked as high as the heavens: skyscrapers of twisted metal, twirling and rotating the ride-goers around in nauseous circles. Those attractions were fun, but they weren't what we were after.

Dad weaved us through the crowds, toward the lineups around the red and white tents, toward the trumpets and the tubas. The flashing lights. This was the true heart of the carnival, Dad used to say, and he would stop at nothing until he won.

He took aim at the water gun tent. Threw his arm out at the wooden blocks. Hucked those plastic rings at the milk bottles. Whacked all of the pesky moles.

I would watch for hours, cheering, waiting to hear the *ding-ding-ding*. When it finally came, he would lift me up and spin me, a smile on his face that would light up the city.

"What does the young lady want?" the Carnie would ask.

I would carefully make my selection from the prizes hanging on the wall.

I chose the stuffed animal every time, the one bigger than myself. Dad would lug it over his shoulder with pride for the rest of the evening.

This same carnival tune, the one synonymous with the circus, I used to skip and pirouette to, through the crowds and the red and white tents. Father and plush animal looking on, in hot pursuit. Now, it brought on panic and horrific nightmares. Things I would never be able to unsee.

The same song, different dance.

❖

A blood-curdling scream sent prickly chills up my spine.

"It's coming! It's coming!" A woman's shrill warning reverberated through the pit. It incited more panicked screams from the others. My heart was banging in my chest, waiting for what's next.

The hum of the hydraulics and the screaming grew louder.

"Rabbit, watch out!"

I felt a sudden fire in my back, followed by a violent scraping. The force flipped my limp body over, sparks flying from the impact. And without warning, the metal claw disappeared back into the air.

Repositioned on my side, I could now see the strange, horrendous environment. Curled-up bodies were scattered everywhere in fetal positions around the base of the pit. They were all in different animal onesies, just their faces poking out of their furry exteriors.

The sheer depth of the pit was staggering; it seemed to go up forever. The enclosure was surrounded by lights, dug into the side of the earth. They lit up the base of the pit. Every five feet or so, there were different rows of lights in red, green, yellow, and blue. They would blink, on and off, in a choreographed pattern with the music. As you got closer to the top, it went black, except for a shallow light in the corner, that if you squinted hard enough, you could make out a glass chute inserted into the earth.

A woman teddy bear was positioned on her side across from me. From the way she was moving, I could tell she was tightly bound like me. Her hands and feet were wrapped together like a straight-jacket cocoon. The sewn-on hands and legs of the bear flopped as she struggled to reposition. Our faces were now in line, maybe three feet away from each other.

"You're bleeding, Rabbit," she said, a grim look upon her face.

My insides cringed as I saw the blood pooling underneath me. Scarier than the blood was the lack of pain.

She shifted slightly. "Don't worry about the paralysis. The feeling should come back in a few hours. At least it did for most of us." She glanced up, "Worry about that thing. It's coming back... and soon."

A loud gasp from the room confirmed her fear. As the lights danced, the metal claw came crashing down again, landing inches from my helpless body. This time it had collected someone in its grasp: a woman with raggedy, chocolate hair. The shark's fins and tail bobbed up and down as she was lifted into the air.

As she was carried up in stiff, robotic movements, the others were breathing heavy sighs of relief. The arm retracted into the sky, into the darkness, then jerked to the right corner of the pit, dropping her body down into the glass chute. Her screams disappeared with her.

The room went still. The colored lights flicked off, and you could feel the release of tension.

The teddy bear smiled beside me. "Congratulations, Rabbit. You survived your first round."

The music continued. But soon after the lights turned off, the sound of a spray nozzle could be heard. Mist shot through tiny puncture holes in the dirt.

And everything went black.

I learned to adapt.

Eventually, the paralysis wore off, but a sharp, stabbing pain took its place. The claw had cut into me—deep; but when I peered over my shoulder, I could see some repair work had been completed. No one knew how long the mist knocked you out for. They only knew everything reset. New victims were added. The place was cleaned.

I learned that once you awoke from the mist, you should head straight toward the food. Food and water were filled to the brims in large containers near the corner of the pit. First come, first serve. We would maneuver around the troughs and devour the sloppy mix of corn, beans, and unrecognizable mush. You learned to love the mush. Like a group of maggots bobbing up and down around the insides of a rancid carcass, feeding time was the highlight of your day.

Eventually, your body would digest the slop. You could only hold it in for so long. Squirming around in your own warm excrement was never fun, but you learned to live with the smell. And once the mist came, you knew you would wake up and feel clean once again. If you managed to survive the round.

◈

Time didn't exist in the pit. You learned to live with its absence.

In my normal life, I was a slave to my schedule: 9:00am-5:00pm at the office, dinner at 6:00pm, and bedtime at 10:00pm. Time dictated everything, and there never seemed to be enough of it. Now, time was in abundance. It was dangerous having so much of it. You pondered all of the mistakes you made in your life. All of the good things you let slip away. Everything, big or small, that you took for granted.

In the pit, instead of time, people kept track of the rounds they survived. One day I asked Carrie why people cared about their number. She spoke about her twelve rounds like it was a badge of honor.

"Why do you want to stay in this hell hole?" Don't you want to get... chosen?"

She pondered for a moment, then glanced up to the sky. "I don't know what's waiting up there." She paused. "I know that down here, though, in the pit, is where the humanity is." She winked, "And us girls need to stick together."

Carrie's snow-white head of hair blended in with the polar bear suit she was wearing. She had this caring glimmer in her eyes that reminded me of Grandma.

She looked into my eyes, forehead crinkled, "Just don't ever give up, dear. Fight. Stay hidden in the corners. There's gotta be someone out there, someone out there looking for us."

I gave a faint smile.

That's when I decided to spend my time getting to know the others. It kept my mind off of the past and away from the impending doom. And together, we made each other stronger and kept each other optimistic.

Carrie made it nineteen rounds before it finally got her.

She yelled, "I love you girls!" before she managed to squeeze her way out of the claw's grip.

The claw was too high. And she was falling too fast.

Nineteen rounds. The longest anyone has ever lasted.

The teddy bear's name was Tanya. She was a rough-around-the-edges trucker from Missouri. The type of person who took no two shits from anyone, but you could tell underneath her hard exterior, she had a kind soul. She went on about her two daughters. She would take the family on the road with her while she worked and still found time to homeschool them after her shifts. If she had access to her arms, she would have reached into her purse and showed off photos of her children.

"The life's not for everyone," she smiled. "But if you can handle the long hours, the money's great. And I got paid to travel with my family. Really nothing better if you ask me." She stopped for a moment before continuing, "So, Rabbit, you got any kids?"

"The name's Amela," I replied.

I thought for a little while before answering. I considered myself a lot of things before the pit, but I never considered myself a mother. When I found out I had ovarian cancer, all my loved ones looked at me like I had a death sentence. They began to handle me with kid gloves. Their conversational tone changed. Mom would leave the room on most occasions in a fit of tears.

The doctors gave me a twenty percent chance to live. If I survived, there was a high chance that the chemotherapy would render me infertile. It was rough. But to be honest, I wasn't too bothered about the infertility. Roger and I, we just weren't *those* kind of people. Kids were never a part of our plan.

The day I found out I was in remission was the happiest day of my life. Roger and I decided to finally get serious: we set a date and got married by the lake. We traveled across Europe. Bought a Golden Retriever. Did everything we'd always wanted to do but had pushed aside for tomorrow. One night, Roger turned over in bed and said something that rattled me:

"I think we should try for one, Amz."

I threw all the excuses I could at him: how our work schedules were too hectic, how we never wanted to be like our parents, how our lives would forever change, the sacrifices we would have to make. But he never wavered. Eventually, it became clear that if I didn't have a baby, I would lose him. So, I agreed. I thought maybe this cancer experience had changed us, maybe we were finally ready to bring a little one into the world.

And then precious Erica came into our lives, an absolute miracle. And it became clear that we weren't ready. That we were never going to be ready.

Everyone close to us had stories about how amazing it was to be a parent, how fulfilling the experience had been, and how they wouldn't trade it for the world. We heard no stories about their regrets: the mourning of the lives they used to have. In the pit of my stomach, I knew I was never wired for motherhood. No experience could have ever changed that, no matter how persuasive Roger was.

The novelty wore off quickly for Roger too. Eventually, we split, and he took a job in New York City. I was left with beautiful Erica, who deserved so much more than I could ever give her.

"... and, no. I don't have any children."

Dad was obsessed with games, in all shapes and forms. He used to tell me it was because they were a microcosm for life. Whether it was a card game, board game, carnival game, or video game, they all required a varying level of skill, strategy, and luck in order for you to win. There was a goal. There were rules you had to follow in order to reach the end. If you completed certain tasks, then you'd win. If you didn't, then you'd lose. To my dad, life was simple. You either won or you lost.

As I got older, I didn't share the same appreciation for games.

Life wasn't simple. There were no "rules" to follow for success. I began to grow frustrated with the inequity and ambiguity in the world. I felt like some people grew up already winning, while others never had a sniff of a chance.

As an adult, I learned that there were a lot of different paths in life. I learned that if I did "A", it did not necessarily lead to "B". One could devote their entire life to reaching the top of their profession but have no friends or family to call their own.

I began to struggle to define what was winning and losing in the real world.

Dad loved all types of games, but his favorites were the ones you were supposed to lose. The ones where the odds were stacked against you. The ones others called "rigged".

As I got older, he would spend hours at the casino. He split his time between the blackjack and roulette tables, testing how far his luck would take him.

My dad bet my family's future on a feeling. The dopamine rush of hitting jackpot.

My dad was a loser. And we lost everything.

But in life, I believe there are more than just winners and losers. I believe there is another category in the grey: for the people who stick around, who just get by no matter the circumstance.

I call those people the survivors.

The young panda's name was Sadie. She was a preacher's daughter. She was currently taking business courses at a Christian community college. She had faith, attending church bright and early every Sunday. She told us that our suffering was part of God's plan, even if none of us could see the meaning in the chaos. In another life, she would have found a nice boy by now and been married, maybe with a little one on the way. Instead, she was in a pit, swapping stories with the rest of the plush animals.

"It was late. I had just finished my Thursday night class. I was sitting on the bench outside the bus terminal, waiting. No one else was around. I was neck-deep in a textbook, cramming for a final I had the following morning." She swallowed. "I didn't see it happen at all. I only felt it—a sharp prick in my shoulder. Then the world faded..."

There was a long pause as despairing glances were shared between everyone in the circle. A sorrowful zoo of misfit animals. We were digesting her story and thinking of Gloria: the elephant that had just been taken away. Tanya reckoned she had lasted ten rounds or so.

"What about you, Amela?" Sadie asked. "What's your last memory before the pit?"

It felt so long ago, my memory foggy, but I tried my best to recall the moment:

"I remember the bastard's face. He was tanned. Armenian or some sort of Middle Eastern. He had slicked-back hair. It was black or maybe dark brown?" I could feel my knuckles clench as I continued, "I got off work late. I was in the convenience store parking lot around midnight, putting my bags away in the trunk of my car." I paused, looking the rest of the captives in their eyes. "You know when you feel someone looking at you? Just an itch, really.

Like there's someone behind you that shouldn't be, someone that's getting too close."

The group nodded.

"Well, I felt that creep behind me, but I ignored it. Pushed it away until it was too late. He jabbed me in the back, but not before I got a good look at him." I smiled, a sadistic smile. "I managed to scratch the fucker a bit before I went out. I bet the bastard doesn't even remember. I hope it cut deep, though. I hope it scarred."

The group chuckled at the minor victory.

I left out the part where I was at the store that night for my daughter. I was gathering supplies to bake her a cake. It was her fifth birthday the following afternoon. My plan was to swoop in and surprise her at Grandma's. I had decided I was ready to try again and was going to take her on full-time.

⬣

The lights started their dance. The hum of the claw fired up as it jerked left and then right, realigning its position.

"It's coming!" I hollered.

The claw shot down from the rooftop like lightning, the metal blades slicing at the floor. Blood spurted out like a mini geyser as a fox flailed in the air. Deafening shrieks of terror filled the room. Impaled through the stomach, the body rose with the blades, the bushy tail waving goodbye with every jerk. As the claw retracted, the body slipped off the blade, plunging to the ground with a thunderous thud.

I never got to know the green-eyed fox. She was an unfortunate new recruit.

Like a whip, the claw snapped back, aiming for another target. My blood boiled when I saw the black and white bear in its grasp.

"Sadie, No!"

You could see the whites of Sadie's eyes as if she had seen a ghost. She shrieked. As she rose higher, her screaming turned into quiet mumbling.

"*Our Father, who art in heaven…*"

"Stay strong, Sadie!" Tanya bellowed through tears.

We watched her lift into the sky and drop down the chute.

That night we said a prayer for young Sadie.

When the claw finally took me, I was ready, accepting of my fate. I flinched as the blades closed in and wrapped around me, luckily centered on my body so nothing was punctured or impaled.

"Amela!" Tanya cried. Her face was a runny mess of tears and agony. The arm slowly jerked its way to the chute. I could feel my body shaking from a mix of nerves and rage. To the left of the chute, I could see the glass panels. There were silhouettes staring back at me in control of the claw.

I didn't know what was on the other side waiting for me, but I knew I was ready to fight.

I shot down the chute like a kid down a waterslide. I tumbled into a dark room with screens and flashing lights.

"Hello?"

No answer.

I squirmed to my feet, waiting in the darkness.

The door creaked open, and then the lights were switched on. The man grinned, quickly closing the door behind him. His baggy dress shirt, gold chain, and slicked-back hair stood before me.

"Let me go you piece of shit," I said, hopping closer toward him. The room was filled with screens playing preloaded arcade games and pinball machines around the perimeter. The place looked like a lonely Dave and Busters.

"Congratulations," he snickered.

"I said, let me go. You sick fuck."

"Easy, bitch," he snarled back. "Don't go pushing your luck." He opened the door. "He still has to collect his prize."

A chubby teenager with a thick neck walked through. He smelled of smoked meat and was dressed in shorts and a skin-tight Paw Patrol shirt. "Okay, Billy. Grab your prize." A crooked smile spread across the businessman's face. It was the face of a man who appeared to be just as obsessed with games as my father.

I swung my neck, the side of my head smashing into the greasy man's nose. There was a satisfying crunch.

The teenager dressed like a boy fumbled some words out of his mouth, "Daddy... Toy?"

"You bitch!" the man mumbled under his breath, blood seeping out of his nose. He wiped the blood and snot onto his sleeve and softened his tone. "Yes, Billy. Go grab your toy. It's time to play."

The man jabbed a needle into my thigh, and the world began to blur.

I could see the bulge in Billy's pants, the fat rolls seeping out of his shirt. The oaf's eyes lit up as he skipped excitedly toward me. He lugged me over his broad shoulders with pride.

"When you're done playing with that one, we can get you a new prize!" the man promised.

At that moment, I knew. I wasn't a winner or a loser.

As we left and everything faded, I knew.

I was a survivor.

❖

I woke up in an alleyway, a broken toy. The ghost of what happened to me haunting my soul.

My body had been badly beaten, my head groggy, my confidence shook.

But a sick part of me was grateful. The game was finally over.

I waited in the cold for the paralysis to wear off, lying facedown on the pavement. Once my faculties slowly came back, I knew.

I had to get back to Erica. And then we would find the others.

PRISONER 1N54N3

The room had become a relic of the past, an afterthought over the years. The thick velvet walls and loop pile carpet made the space feel like you had traveled back in time: back to a simpler time_when you were just a kid waiting to catch a flick at the local run-down theatre. There was a presence, however, buried within the confines of its walls. Its purpose never forgotten. The space held some significance in the past: reserved as a meeting ground for the finest minds—scientists, pharmacologists, and physicians—to brainstorm and unpack their findings.

Most importantly, it was a place to bear witness to their final moments.

To, hypothetically, say goodbye to the unfortunate soul on the other side. The words trapped in the sound-proof walls, never to be delivered.

These days, the room housed a lowly lab assistant, like myself, and the occasional physician passing through. Things had changed, and rather quickly. Use of the observational lair had declined once the studies steadily progressed. When the facility was upgraded, it was deemed more cost-effective to leave the room as is rather than tear it down. The space was left_to effectively collect dust. Any new breakthroughs were largely kept quiet and run up the appropriate chain of command.

I found I could get a lot done in the room. It was a quiet place to lay your hat, take notes, and more importantly, reflect.

However, today, it was far from quiet.

I was too tired to deal with a crowd today. *It's the work*, I told myself. It had to be the work. No one could see what I had seen and come out unscathed; it had finally begun to take its toll. Each day felt shorter and shorter, the absence of time wrestling with my brain at night.

Jean, on the other hand, looked unchanged. She entered, waving to me from across the room. I soaked her in as she walked toward me, her straight hair bouncing with every step. Her smile radiated with an all-encompassing zest, a youthfulness that had passed me by. I knew too much now. But still, I yearned for that feeling once again.

"Some spectacle, huh?" I winked.

Every seat opposite the one-way mirror was occupied, the tiny space cramped with camera equipment propped up along the aisles. A low, excited murmur was shared between those in lab coats, wooly sweaters, and three-piece suits. Their faces were unblemished, their hair waxy and smooth without so much of a stray strand out of place. Most eerie was their skin tone—it seemed to *sparkle* like a layer of glitter had been sprinkled upon their perfect skin. Their smiles stretched wide in warm, familiar grins.

It was quite the occasion for them, indeed.

Jean's soft hand patted my shoulder. "Hi, Wayne. How are you doing?"

I nodded back and smiled. Removing my notepad from the seat beside_me, I motioned for her to sit. "Doesn't it feel... I don't know. Wrong to you?" I asked.

"What does?"

I sighed. Jean's memory had been getting worse. I couldn't fault her for it, it could have been a side effect of the experiments.

There was no telling what they did to her, what they fed her, when she was all alone. I prayed it wasn't half as bad as what they did to me.

"This whole place," I remarked.

Jean thought about it for a moment. She rummaged through her messenger bag and pulled out her clipboard. In the process, she handed me a pen. "It does, doesn't it?" She paused, writing something in her notebook.

I began to scribble in mine, as well. Mostly a nervous doodle—I had a tendency to do that.

"You ever catch yourself feeling guilty?" I asked.

It was an honest question, one I often grappled with myself. I wasn't expecting a groundbreaking response—it wasn't like there were other options—but Jean offered nothing in return. She appeared to be somewhere else, her vacant stare drifting off into the distance.

After some time, she snapped out of her daze. "It will be over, soon enough," she declared in a somber tone.

My nervous doodling continued. I shrugged, "It will never be over."

Dr. Harper was one of the most respected physicians on the planet, but I_didn't always agree with his decisions. On this occasion, I felt he fell victim to the pressures of the outside world. The work wasn't over, and yet he had decided to put an end to a chapter, forever. This was unnecessary, in my opinion. The man still deserved respect, despite what many others (including the doctor) would say.

I caught a tear running down Jean's cheek; she tried her best to disguise the wipe as a scratch. Jean understood the harsh reality just as much as I did. I had trusted her as a confidant, a loyal friend, and a trusty associate for years. She had been briefed on all the cases. Still, I felt out of place offering comfort in the murky waters of her personal boundaries; so I pretended to ignore the emotional slip-up, kept my head down, and continued my doodles.

"Quite a long time to keep us waiting," I said.

"*Oh*, before I forget—" Jean reached into her bag and pulled out a styrofoam container. The aroma washed over the room. I could hardly contain the saliva pooling in my mouth: a heaping cut of tenderloin, creamy mashed potatoes, and a side of vegetables. She handed me the spork before I passed out.

"Geez, Jean. I'm not complaining... but what's this for?" The combination of my workload and the commotion of the crowd seemed to have distracted me from the rumbling in my stomach.

"For *you*," she winked.

The meal caught the eye of an envious few across the room. I craned my neck slightly, motioning back at the onlookers. "I better chomp this down before it ensues a riot over here. You want some?"

She furrowed her brows, a look of unease across her face. "Nope, all yours. Enjoy."

I ate quickly, shoveling the contents into my mouth like the meal would be my last. In the process, a speck of gravy dripped onto the side of my pocket. I cursed under my breath and wiped it as best I could, admiring how Jean always kept her lab coat so pristine.

Through a mouthful of potatoes, I spat out, "Well, totally unnecessary, Jean. But thank you. This is a feast fit for a king."

"Enjoy."

Some days were filled with heavy dread. All of them should have been insufferable. But Jean had always managed to find a way to shed little rays of light into the darkness. A silly photo here, a funny news article there. Her assignment to me had been a blessing, the only shed of humanity the facility had shown me over the years.

A hush hissed from the crowd as the curtain was pulled open.

He marched slowly, the chains dragging on the floor with every step. Shackles bounded his hands and feet. I wondered when was the last time the sun had braised his skin, his body whiter than a coconut's flesh.

"Spare the man some dignity," I groaned to Jean.

They stripped the dark garments off of the man's body, his daisy-white ass exposed to the crowd.

Her attention shifted from her notebook, to me, and then finally to the window. "Oh gosh. Remind me of the file number again?"

This case she forgets? I thought. *The case of all cases.* I rolled my eyes. "Jean, this is Aubuckner. You should remember him."

Her palm shot to her forehead. "Oh, forgive me. How foolish of me, Wayne. Sorry. Hardly recognized him there."

It was a testament to all of the subjects we had studied. All of the experiments we had conducted.

"It's been a while since I've heard his name. Is he really still in performatory? Or observatory?"

"Nope," I responded, scraping the last bits of carrots into my mouth. "Judgment day for Mr. Aubuckner."

She inhaled slowly, the gravity of the situation overtaking her. "*Oh*, I see now. That must explain the crowd."

I nodded; my eyes fixated on Aubuckner as they carried his emaciated body to the gurney. He squinted as the bright beams of light illuminated his pale skin. Every mole, every roll of skin on display. The man seemed incredibly calm considering what he was about to endure.

While Aubuckner was being strapped in, Dr. Harper washed his hands in the metal sink. Another doctor prepared a row of instruments and laid out the small, packaged materials on the metal counter.

The viewing area stayed quiet; the crowd hunched forward in their seats. Jean stared back at me. "What's wrong?"

I offered very little in response, just a subtle shake of my head.

I thought of Nuremberg. Unit #731. I couldn't argue against us being any different. Under the guise of longevity research, so many lines had been blurred that it was hard to pinpoint where it all went wrong. But it all started with this man, Aubuckner, the first to have signed up willingly for the experiments. I had watched him take every dose, every mixture under the blood-red sun that you could think of. There were very few veins that hadn't been touched. It took a lot of throwing shit at the wall before a combination was discovered that had any trace of success. At that time, I was hopeful for the project. Some might have called me naive.

He was a young, uneducated man in need of money. They all were. And that was the problem. You scoop up a man in that predicament and there's not a lot he will turn down. And sure, he had requested to leave multiple times once the side effects had kicked in. Once his skin began to glow and his wrinkles vanished. On the outside, he looked beautiful. On the inside, it was another story. But at that point, it was too far gone. We needed to understand the side effects and collect the data in order to maximize efficiency.

When I discovered he and some of the others were being held captive, I threatened to leave. I was prepared to blow the whistle on the whole project. That's when they turned me into a captive too. I was deemed dangerous. A flight risk. At least until the final mixture was discovered... the holy grail of vitality research.

The compound for eternal life.

Until then... I still had value. Aubuckner, however, had very little to offer anymore. He looked nothing of his former self: his muscle tone, his liveliness, had been drained from him long ago. No one knew what happened to the glow, but it eventually disappeared.

I held a soft place in my heart for the man because people would never know his name. They would reap the benefits of his sacrifices without any knowledge of the history.

Dr. Harper pulled on some latex gloves while another doctor adjusted the elevation of the gurney.

Over the intercom, Dr. Harper spoke with a deep, monotone voice:

"Good evening, Darryl Aubuckner."

Aubuckner stared straight back at us through the glass with no discernable reaction.

Dr. Harper slowly outlined the stages of the process to Aubuckner while his assistants hurriedly prepared the room: the first drug to be administered was pentobarbital in order to render him unconscious, the second, pancuronium bromide, would result in his paralysis, and the final compound, potassium chloride, would be the one to stop his heart.

Aubuckner's blank stare never wavered.

"You've been of great service to the world, Mr. Aubuckner. Your contributions will live on forever."

He turned his head and spat in the doctor's direction, the loogie landing smack dab in the middle of his face mask. The chunky snot oozed down the plastic shield to the floor.

"Charming," the doctor replied, turning toward the back of the room. He replaced his mask and gloves with a fresh set. The process was delayed a couple of minutes, but Dr. Harper returned, unmoved.

He asked the old man, "Any final words?"

Aubuckner's eyes flared in his direction before returning to the glass. "I'll see you all in hell."

The intercom cut off as we watched the scenes unfold. Dr. Harper inserted the IV and administered the first dose into the man's arm. After a few moments, Aubuckner's body began to tremble. The second drug was issued, and the man's face began to change: it twisted with anguish, his teeth gritted together, the veins on his neck bulging in thick blue knots. He opened his mouth to scream, and spittle cascaded out of the opening.

I turned away, grimacing.

Still, with no hesitation, Dr. Harper prepared the final dose and proceeded to insert it into Aubuckner. The old man jolted as the last of the_syringe emptied into his bloodstream. He was still shaking as his eyes slowly closed.

The crowd gasped.

Dr. Harper and his assistants had already begun to dispose of the waste, but even from our distance, we could make out the physical changes occurring in Aubuckner. His eyes were still shut, but his eyelids were flickering in quick tiny bursts like a hummingbird's fluttering wings. Most astonishing was his skin: it started slowly from his face and then moved throughout his body. He was *glowing* with tiny speckles that shined a bright golden-honey, the shimmer of a hundred polished diamonds.

Without warning, his eyes opened, and the man lurched forward. His arms flailed wildly, testing the limits of the straps. Dr. Harper leapt from the sink, the tap still running. The others in the chamber dropped what they were doing and rushed toward Aubuckner, who was now gyrating his head around like the rotor blades of a helicopter. They tried to pull his arms down, leaning on the straps of the gurney, while Dr. Harper fled to the back of the room.

The intercom kicked in—a horrifying mixture of screams and static. The bellowing from Aubuckner was guttural, it shook the speakers in tremendous, whooping wails.

I covered my ears. Jean wrapped an arm around me.

"Are you okay, Wayne?"

The bellowing intensified, rattling my eardrums with the force of an air horn. I closed my eyes and begged for it to stop.

Please put him out of his misery.

The screaming continued, the assistants struggling to hold Aubuckner down. In one moment, Dr. Harper had a vial in his hand; in the next, he was scrambling back to the supply cabinet to fish out supplies, and then shuffling back to the counter to fidget with the sealed packages.

"Wayne, it's okay," Jean said soothingly. "It's okay."

There was one final shriek; and like a needle had been lifted from a dusty record player, there was abrupt silence.

Then came the knocking: three loud bangs from behind.

I opened my eyes, and it was as if a light had been flicked on, and in its place, a new reality surfaced. The dim orange hue fizzled out and was replaced by a blinding white light. The room was a padded white cube. The crowd had dissipated into thin air, leaving only the three of us: Jean, the doctor, and myself.

"It's time, Mr. Winslow," Dr. Harper said, stepping forward from the shadows of the doorway. He had his surgical cap atop his head, his words muffled by the mask.

"Wait... please!" I pleaded. "We almost have it! We're almost there!" The doctor pointed in my direction. Two guards entered and marched toward me. They hoisted me up from my armpits. During the struggle, I sunk my teeth into one of their arms. Blood ran down my lips, the taste of metal in my mouth.

"You animals! You deserve to burn in the fiery depths of hell, you wretched fucks! Look at what you've done! You will pay for these sins!" The cuffs around my ankles scraped against the padded floor like a desperate cat trying to claw his way out.

The glass no longer revealed the other side. Maybe the other side was looking in?

I caught something else, in flickers, as I wrestled for my survival. The crowd had resurfaced. They were applauding as I fought to break free. Their faces no longer sparkled, they were now covered in filth: dirt, grime, and flakes of dark blood. Their outfits were tattered, barely clinging to their skin. Where some were missing limbs, others had open wounds the size of tennis balls. Flaps of filleted flesh flopped from their abdomens as their palms slapped together in glee. Aubuckner was front row, clapping the loudest. One of his eyes was missing where only a mangled socket of burnt skin tissue remained.

The intercom crackled above: *Code black. Cellblock nine.*

Backup flooded into the room, their arms wrapped around me.

"Jean, destroy the files!" I urged.

Her face was now awash in tears, her body shaking. She followed behind, handing her notebook to Dr. Harper. Her access card dangled from her front pocket. Through trembling lips, she managed to mouth back:

I'm sorry.

◆

January 19th, 2023.

Dr. Wayne Winslow.
Convicted of fifteen counts of first-degree murder and torture.
Time of execution: 7:13PM.

AZALEA'S COOKHOUSE

Part I: The Promotion

"Azalea's Cookhouse. How can I help you?"

I despised the inflection in my voice, the fakeness irked me to my core. But it was all part of the job, and I took my customer service seriously.

I've been a waiter for longer than I'm comfortable admitting. And although the job isn't rocket science by any stretch, I believe there are skills one needs to develop in order to be successful: a wide smile, a cheery demeanor, and an unhealthy tolerance for bullshit. If you made sure everyone's waters were filled and remembered to ask about dessert before bringing back the bill, you would do well in this profession. The tricks of the trade were simple. But you'd be surprised how many college kids wandered into the industry with zero regard for service. It was an epidemic, as far as I was concerned. Pretty faces were always welcome, but seldom did they stay.

It wasn't like this was my dream job, either. I used to have real ambitions. I played in a rock band. I had a marriage. Those things, well, I wish they were as simple. When everything went up in flames, when it all started to slip away, the restaurant industry was always there, and to them, I was valuable.

A place like Azalea's was a great gig. They demanded a pristine level of service or your ass was kicked to the curb, but for what you got paid compared to other competitors, I felt the trade-off was worth it.

"Hello. I'd like to make a reservation for Friday evening."

I recognized the silky voice right away. It was a twist of warm friendship mixed with passionate lover. It was elegant and upbeat.

It was Paulina.

I didn't take my neighbor for the type to dine at this kind of establishment. And while it was only her voice—she could have been a million miles away—it was enough to send me into an anxious tailspin.

"Hello?"

"Uhh... sorry, ma'am. That's not a problem. And for how many?"

"Four, please."

In less than a minute, it was confirmed. She was scheduled for tomorrow at 7:00PM. *That* voice. Oh, that voice... it had reduced me to a teenager again. Visions of her watering her flowers and walking her dog occupied my mind for the rest of the evening.

Paulina was in her front yard in the morning, meticulously tending to a healthy bed of flowers. She smiled from a crouched-over position, her golden hair adding to the splashes of flourishing color: tulips, sunflowers, and geraniums were spread thick across the lawn like a rainbow nestled in a sky of green.

We exchanged waves—her mouth open and ready for conversation—just as the back gate swung open. All at once, they were upon her in an orchestrated attack. Concentrated streams of water blasted out of the barrel of their guns. She let out a wail, shielding her face from the onslaught. Her white tank top was now see-through, drenched by the precision of trained killers. The shooters—her two sons and husband, Keith,—were giggling at the scene of the crime as her pleas for mercy went unanswered.

I kept on walking.

◈

"Hey, Marc."

I waved to the group with a slight smile. A couple of the waiting staff were huddled together in front of the stairs that led into the restaurant. It was their ceremonious drag of nicotine before the chaos; Friday evenings were always a gong show, and this one was sure to be no exception. One of the busboys, Dewayne, was wearing a vexed look on his face. After his puff, he warned me:

"Silva is looking for you, man."

I nodded and made my way to the entrance. "Appreciate the heads up."

From the outside, you could never tell Azalea's was a restaurant. It looked more like a cellar with cracked cement stairs that led down into a basement. That was Silva's vision all along: to be a hidden diamond in the rough. Walk in thinking the place was a dump, walk out pleasantly surprised. It was the psychology of the food industry, and this element of surprise seemed to be essential for fine dining.

Azalea's was the height of exclusivity, not just anyone could stumble in. In order to keep up this allure, speaking about the restaurant in any capacity was strictly prohibited. Staff were never allowed to dine-in. We were servants, not clientele. Not that any of us could afford it—the menu items never seemed to reference a price, which always signaled trouble—but from the bills I'd hand out at the end of every meal the numbers were always staggering. It was clear Azalea's was catering to a very specific crowd with refined tastes and deep pockets.

A referral and a reservation got you through the door. You needed both. No exceptions.

This drew a certain type of crowd. Snooty. High maintenance. But I didn't mind it, to be honest. That combination could be tiresome, but it usually meant great tips.

I approached the splintered door and knocked three times. One of the greeters let me in.

The interior was nothing like the exterior: the foyer had a gothic-medieval vibe with high ceilings and narrow hallways. Chandeliers sparkled overhead in the dim light. The halls were plastered with stone and exposed brick, a handful of doors on either side. The doors concealed the intimate dining experience that Azalea's offered: private rooms for every party to make you feel at home. Silva's office was the last door on the left.

I knocked with caution. No response.

Two more times—nothing.

Confused, I headed back the way I came.

"Hey, Julie. Have you seen Silva around? Dewayne said he was looking for me?"

The greeter glanced up from her tablet. "Hey. No, haven't seen him." Her eyes dived back into the seating chart on the screen. Workers were starting to enter now, squeezing past us down the hall.

"If you see him, can you please let him know I went to his office?"

She nodded.

I followed the flow of traffic toward the change rooms. My shift was about to start, and I needed to set the tables before dinner service.

❖

The night became a flurry of well-dressed people and trips to the kitchen. I scuttled past the maze of bodies into narrow pockets of space while balancing wobbly plates of delectable food. Just another day at the circus.

There were glimpses of Silva here and there, darting across the halls with his scruffy beard and velvet blazer. He was bouncing from employee to customer to his office like a bad game of pong. I didn't bother seeking him out; I knew that he would come and find me when there was time for a breath of air.

In the middle of me reaming out a busboy, Paulina strode past. Her maxi dress sparkled with little rhinestones, flowing with the natural curves of her body, leaving nothing to the imagination. It appeared to be a family affair tonight: the boys looked dapper in their matching bow ties, and Keith was all smiles in his tailored suit. This was a special occasion, indeed.

"Marc?"

My heart sank as she disappeared into one of the rooms. One of the rooms I wasn't working.

Martin's voice rattled my ears. "Marc? Are you deaf, man? Earth to Marc! You're in my bloody way."

"You can fuck off tonight, Martin. Not tonight. I don't answer to you."

He rolled his eyes and I glared back at the lethargic slug. The man looked like he hadn't caught a wink of sleep in years; his bags were a deep black like a coat of mascara had been slathered under his eyes. I rattled the massive cart he was leaning against, the weight shifting in a dangerous, teetering fashion. Some china clattered together with ominous clangs.

"Fuck off!" he yelped.

"You see the problem here?" I quipped. "The quicker you do your job, the quicker this stupid tank of a unit is out of *my* way. You're clogging up the freeway!"

His brows furrowed as he pushed the cart away. The metal contraption was over six feet tall and wide: an ugly, metal cabinet on wheels. His movement was purposefully slow, and he muttered something under his breath as he passed.

"What did you say?" I scowled.

He was near the kitchen before he hollered it back to me in clear English: "It ain't as easy as it looks, chump."

I took a deep breath before entering the adjacent room: "*Welcome to Azalea's!*"

On my way back from the kitchen, I was balancing two plates of Hakarl (an Icelandic delicacy of fermented shark) when Silva tapped me on my shoulder.

"Marc. I need you in my office. Drop those off and come see me, please."

"Umm... It's mid-dinner service, Silva. Can this wait till my break?"

"It can't," he replied. "Lana will cover for you."

My blood boiled at the thought of Lana swooping in to claim my tips. She wasn't even scheduled to work this evening. I sighed and dropped off the food before making my way to his office. This time the three knocks were answered; the door swung open.

"Thanks, Marc. Have a seat."

We were surrounded by a forest of cherry wood: bookshelves and cabinets along the perimeter, carved in looping, intricate patterns. Everything was polished and quaint. There were floating shelves that carried up the walls, each holding rows and rows of books. Behind a grandfather clock in the corner were pots of leafy plants. I wondered how any of them survived in this dungeon.

"You've been doing a great job here, Marc. I know I'm not the most 'rah-rah' type of owner, but believe me when I say this, I've taken notice." He continued, the sounds of muffled conversation trickling in through the halls, "I'll level with you here—I'm in a bit of a pickle. We are short busboys tonight. I need you to cover."

"Uh... with all due respect, Silva, why would I do that?"

"Because I need you to, Marc. And to be honest, it's a chance at a promotion."

A *promotion*? I couldn't get Martin and his multiple smoke breaks out of my mind.

"Look, Silva. I like what I do. I feel like I do it well. I think you'd agree. Now, I'm not saying I don't want to help you out, but please don't spit on my face and tell me it's raining." I sighed heavily in my chair. "I'm a waiter, not a busboy."

"What if I told you the pay was nearly triple?" A smirk grew on his face as he detected my astonishment. He pointed his finger at me, "This doesn't leave the room."

The news went down the hatch like sour milk. I understood why the chefs would make more money—the menu was constantly revolving to keep the clientele happy. They likely had years of experience overseas with a resume that included culinary school. But the *busboys*? I couldn't believe it. These guys were glorified dishwashers.

I knew the way Silva ran the restaurant was different, but this corporate structure was completely backwards. Servers were the face of the business: the point of contact between the restaurant and the customer. Surely that had to hold more value.

"I need you out there, Marc. Like yesterday." He got up and made his way to the door. "If you do well, the position is permanently yours."

"Do I really have a choice?"

"Not really," he laughed, a glint of something conspicuous in his eyes. The door was now ajar, the bustle of the business now flooding into the room. "You'll do great, I know it. Now go and find Dewayne, he'll be showing you the ropes."

Dewayne was outside with one of the chefs, another cigarette to his lips. The light emanating from the lamppost highlighted his bronze complexion.

"Hey, Dewayne," I smiled. "Silva said you are meant to train me tonight or something?"

He raised an eyebrow and dropped the cigarette to the pavement. With a blank expression, he replied: "Well, hot damn. Congrats." He stomped the butt out and we drifted inside.

I followed him deep into the kitchen, past the cooking staff carefully preparing the meals. The atmosphere wasn't much better back there: plates were sliding around amidst fits of yelling and chopping. I passed one of the chefs giving a lecture to one of her apprentices:

"Who taught you how to work a knife? You leave skin on this fugu again, and I'll rip your apron off myself!"

He stopped at one of the metal monstrosities in the corner of the dishroom.

"Get pushing," he instructed.

The cart was frustrating to maneuver given the state of its back wheels: one wheel refused to roll in line with the others, opting to wiggle uselessly instead. It was a cumbersome task given the sheer size of the cart: it was heavy with its many drawers, and it was a challenge seeing over it. There would have certainly been a collision without Dewayne guiding me along. We finally stopped in front of one of the rooms, my arms and legs feeling like jelly. He held the door open as I inched the cart in. Then the door firmly closed shut.

The scene at the dinner table nearly knocked me off my feet.

We were inside the private room that Paulina's family had dined in. There was Keith, his cheek resting in a thin layer of cream sauce. His mouth was full of foam, the tablecloth soaked in a puddle of vomit. His eyes were fixed upon us with a dead stare. Their two sons were on the floor, their bodies lying limp.

There was no ounce of recoil from Dewayne; he gripped Keith's head and pulled it out of the sauce. "Let's go, Marc. We don't got all day."

The walls felt like they were closing in on me. Everything was spinning. "Dewayne... What the fuck is this, man?"

He was dragging Keith by his shoulders, his limp legs bobbling against the ground as he was carried toward the cart. Most of his body was able to fit into one of the compartments, the rest of the parts that overhung were forced in with a metal pole. The squishing and cracking made my stomach churn.

"Well, shit. What did you think this was, Marc? A six-figure dishwashing job?" He laughed, a glint of madness in his eyes. He had one of the boys by the back of his blazer and was dragging him along.

"I'm out. I want nothing to do with this," I declared, turning toward the door. Dewayne dropped the body and beat me there. His arm held the door shut.

"Listen. This might not be for you. I get it, it ain't for everybody." He paused, inching closer. "But listen to me, and listen good. Silva doesn't just let you out."

"I didn't ask for any of this," I yelped. "I'm just a waiter."

"Quite frankly, I'm surprised," he chuckled, shaking his head. "Silva keeps the wait staff soft. All be damned."

"Let me out," I demanded.

"Listen," he urged, "you're a part of the Azalea family. You've just been given a seat at the big boy table. And families—they have secrets." He eased off the door. "Go ahead. Get some fresh air. I'll prep this room, and you can meet me at the front for the next one."

I took off in a steady march past the greeters and guests waiting to be seated, past the menacing stare of Silva. I was focused on one thing—escaping.

The air outside was crisp, it helped steady the spinning. I slowed down to catch my breath, but the rapid gasps for air wouldn't stop.

I'll find a new job, I thought. *Start fresh. Flee the city.*

At the end of the parking lot, something shimmered that caught my eye. It was the flowing dress of Paulina. She was just entering her minivan. I stared at the vehicle as it backed out of the stall and slowly cruised in my direction. Instead of taking the left turn to exit the lot, the van stopped. The window lowered with a mechanical buzz.

"Marc?"

My words were caught in my throat; all I could offer was a slight nod. "Everything okay?" she asked. "I'm just heading home. Do you need a lift?"

Her voice was nonchalant, with no regard for what she'd done. Because she hadn't done anything, except for enjoy a pleasant meal... the Azalea family took care of the rest.

"Marc!" A voice yelled from the bottom of the stairs.

"I've gotta go..." I replied.

"No worries," she smiled, her grin glistening. Before she rolled up her window, she called back: "Hey—let's grab a bite to eat sometime? What do you think?"

The offer hung in the crisp air.

She drove off in the empty mini-van just as Silva emerged from the bottom of the stairwell. His hand was clutching something in his pocket.

"Break time is over!"

Part 2: The Family

Something deep inside of me told me to run.

It cried for me to take flight, to duck behind the nearest car, to weave in and out of the stalls to safety. My brain convinced me otherwise, however. I stared at my red Prius parked at the back of the lot. It was in Silva's direct line of fire, it would be an easy point-blank shot. Freedom was only steps away, but it might as well have been a thousand miles.

Silva's hand crept out of his pocket and landed on my shoulder. The movement was smooth, but not smooth enough. Polished chrome flashed for a moment then disappeared amongst the folds of his dress shirt, back into the confines of his pocket.

Does he know I saw it? Does he care?

"So, how's the shift going?" he asked, squeezing my deltoid tightly. I was biting my lip so hard I tasted blood. As we made our way down the concrete steps, the words finally stumbled out: "I... I don't think I can do this, Silva."

He paused, taking in a deep breath.

I continued, "I just don't know. I feel sick..."

"That's normal. Don't worry. First day of bussing tends to do that to people." We stopped before the entrance, the sounds of classical music leaking out of the building. He finally let go of my shoulder. "Dewayne is waiting for you at table one."

I pleaded with him further, "I really can't, Silva. Please. Let me go back to serving. I won't say anything to anyone, I promise."

I felt his hand gently guiding me forward. "Finish up your shift and we'll chat."

If there was one thing I knew about Silva, it was that he wasn't much of a "chit-chatter".

He stuck his palm out. "But first—phone."

There was a sinking feeling in my chest as I looked back at Silva. Surely he wasn't serious.

"Hand it over. Before we get going here."

"No way," I replied. "I need it."

"Phone," he growled back. "You'll get it back after your shift."

The soft melodies continued, masking the cold-blooded murder taking place behind the doors.

His face turned blood red, the wrath of Silva nearly upon me. It was a face I'd seldom seen before, a crack in his cool, calm demeanor. "Hand over the phone... Now!"

I laid it in his palm, diffusing the situation. He placed it into his other trouser pocket, next-door neighbors to the pistol. "Thank you. Now let's go."

He knocked three times, his scowl morphing into a cheery grin before the door swung open. Just like that, we were back inside the restaurant. In a matter of seconds one of the kitchen staff had whisked Silva away down the hall. Much of the dinner crowd had dispersed with only a moderate number of people left lingering in quiet conversation. I caught Dewayne's gaze as he leaned against the front desk. He was chatting with one of the other busboys.

"You good?" he asked. The slightest smile stretched across his face, only for a moment, until he caught Silva's gaze out of the corner of his eye. His face instantly went blank as he motioned for me to come with him.

I didn't respond, I only followed.

"Table one looks like it's ready. We've got a quick turnaround, so let's hurry."

My eyes shot back at Dewayne. He casually held the door open. "After you."

You could see the woman from the doorway. Her head was face down, layers of shiny ebony locks fanned out across the table. I detected a hint of fruit mixed with a strong hairspray aroma.

Dewayne hovered around the table, grabbing the wine glass across from the lady and swishing around the remnants left in the cup.

"Drink crowd," he smiled. "This one was a real lightweight."

"What's in the drink?" I asked out of morbid curiosity.

He took a whiff. "Some sort of fruity pinot noir. Probably a mix of elderberry."

"How do you know that?" I asked.

"You ever talked to James or Elsa?"

I shook my head, no. Those were two of the head chefs at Azalea's. I never really mingled much with the kitchen staff.

"Well, if you weren't so stuck up, you'd know," he scoffed. He made his way across the table, collecting some of the cutlery. "The dinner crowd wants the experience: the slow burn, the level of poison that could take hours to set in. With some exceptions, of course." He cleared the glasses off the table and chucked them into one of the plastic bins. "The drink crowd—now they're looking for something different. They want the death to be quick and dirty. Instant with minimal suffering." He lifted the lady's head up from the table and examined her face. Her thick layer of makeup had left a stain on the white tablecloth. There was puddle of drool beneath her chin. "At least that's what I'm told. I can't tell you what she died from, but based on the turnaround here, it was quick."

I wondered how many bodies Dewayne had seen over the years.

"Help me grab her," he ordered. "And don't even think about pussying out this time or I'll let Silva know. We need this room cleared, the next group is coming in ASAP."

So I grabbed one of her shoulders and helped hoist her body up. Her face was a disturbing shade of plum, her eyes staring back in a cloudy, empty gaze. She was pretty, what was left of her. She was maybe in her early forties, way too young to suffer this sort of fate.

"How can you do this man?" I asked. Her petite frame easily slid into the confines of the metal walls.

"I dunno," Dewayne said. "At first, I just really needed the money." He closed the door and locked the panel shut. "After a while, it just becomes another job. You'll get used to it... you'll see." He started pushing the metal cart toward the door.

"These people have families, Dewayne," I snapped. "What we're doing here is criminal."

Dewayne shrugged. "You're overthinking this, Marc." He motioned for me to get the door. "These people had a target on their back. Focus on your job, and you'll be fine. We're just simply disposing of the mess that someone else has made."

With that bleak sentiment, we pushed the cart through the hall in silence. On our way to the kitchen, we passed by the next group of patrons: a couple of young professionals with vibrant smiles and flamboyant suits. My mind played Russian roulette with their bodies—which one would we fetch next?

It was clear that Dewayne had been corrupted. The money, the trauma (maybe a combination of the two) had severely warped his mind into having a morbid indifference for life. I knew my words would go nowhere with him.

I had the business model all wrong. Everything I thought Azalea stood for: quality dining, intimate gatherings, unbeatable service—it was all a lie.

With the dinner crowd dissipating, the halls were a lot quieter and easier to maneuver through.

I knew this was my chance. I knew I had one shot.

Dewayne led the way, pulling the metal cart from the front. I was at the caboose, pushing the heavy contraption ahead as best I could. The towering cart would provide the shelter that I needed. Out of my front pocket, I pulled out a pen and notepad: the trusty tools of the trade. Keeping one hand on the cart and pushing it along, I used the other to frantically scribble together a note. Craning my neck from one side of the cart to the other, I caught a glimpse of Silva. He was on the right side of the hall chatting with one of the guests.

The cart squeaked by as we approached the front of the house. If I timed it right, his view would be blocked, but only for a moment. As we approached the front desk, I took a deep breath and crumpled up the note.

"Julie!" I whispered.

She was alone, her face planted in the tablet. I could feel the opportunity slipping away.

Just as we passed Silva on my right, I had no choice but to gamble. I took aim and lobbed the note into the air. The ball of paper seemed to float as I watched in horror. It overshot the table and ricocheted off Julie's shoulder, just as we passed the front desk and Silva came into view. The impact broke her gaze from the screen. The paper fell to the floor—where it landed, I wasn't quite sure. I caught her annoyed glance in my direction before steadying my attention to the front of the cart. As we exited the front of the house and entered the hallway to the kitchen, I could feel Silva's gaze burning a hole in the back of my skull.

The intensity in the kitchen had also simmered down compared to earlier in the evening. Many of the cooks had gone home, and only a handful of chefs remained, fussing around with the various dessert arrangements. There were plates of chocolate lava cakes topped with caramel drizzle, crème brûlée in little cups with apricot shavings, and some sort of tower of fudge layered with sheets of sugar. The garnish was a colorful display of ackee fruit and lychee. I admired the creativity from afar as we wheeled the cart into the dish room. Dewayne discarded the dirty dishes, and then we pushed the cart around the corner. I saw each chef bring their masterpiece over to Elsa. She inspected everything in the back, added the finishing touches, and then the plates were carried away by the servers.

Dewayne led us down a dark hallway that bore no resemblance to the restaurant. It smelled of musk, and it was left dusty with no attempt made to clean or decorate the area. There were holes in the drywall, cracks in the concrete, and questionable stains on the ceiling. We took the cart as far as we could until we hit a dead end. The only thing at the end of the hall was a service elevator. Dewayne swiped his access card, then hit the button. We waited a couple of moments until we heard a high-pitched *ding*. I half expected a wave of blood to come pouring out like "The Shining". Instead, Martin's ghoulish face popped out.

"Why is this asshole back here?" he asked.

"Silva's orders," Dewayne said. "He's a busboy now."

Martin's lips formed a wry smile. "*Oh*, is he now?"

I looked away and helped push the cart into the elevator. I stepped inside and waited for Martin to hit the button down.

"Nuh-uh," Dewayne said, waving me out. "Only Martin is allowed down."

I stepped out. Martin muttered something under his breath just as the door closed:

"Chump."

◈

The rest of the night carried on like a bad nightmare. I toed the line, collecting the bodies and transporting them to the back of the kitchen. The smell of excrement and death continued to make me gag. Dewayne seemed immune to the scent; he found humor in my reaction after every pickup.

No matter how hard I tried, it was impossible to get their faces out of my head: the bulge of their eyes, the blueish-purple tint of their skin, the bloaty look in their cheeks. Their loved ones would never find them. The gravity of it all was sinking in. When midnight finally hit, I was itching to leave the restaurant. Silva was waiting for me at the exit.

"How did it go?" he inquired, pulling me into his office.

I took a seat. "Nothing's changed, Silva," I said. "The position's not for me."

"Well," he sighed. "I'm disappointed, to say the least..." He went quiet, pacing around the room. "It's going to be hard to find a replacement." He strolled over to one of his plants and inspected the leaves.

I eventually worked up the nerve to cut off the awkward silence. "Can I go home now? My shift's over."

He broke out of his trance and walked over to his desk. In the top drawer, he pulled out my phone and slid it across the table.

"Of course," he replied. "I trust, as always, that this stays inside the family?" The words were cold, his piercing stare a warning in itself.

"Of course," I responded. I got up from my seat and made my way to the door.

"When do you work next, Marc?"

"Monday."

He glanced up from his paperwork, "Have a good weekend."

I held my breath as I walked out of the restaurant, traveling as fast as my feet would take me. Only once I left the parking lot did my nerves return to normal. I was free, and there was only one thing on my mind. I needed to put as many miles as I could between myself and Azalea's. I could find another job, that would be easy, but the victims' families deserved closure, and Silva needed to be exposed as the monster he truly was. I was torn.

One problem was my phone. I tried to swipe and click the power button with no success. As desperately as I wanted to call the cops, the call would have to wait till I got home to my charger.

The streets were quiet as I pulled into the cul-de-sac. The lights were off in every household on the block, the whole neighborhood asleep. Paulina's minivan was parked in her driveway; the sight of the vehicle sent shivers up my spine. Pulling up to my driveway, the headlights revealed something stuck to my garage door. I parked the car and walked over to inspect the object. It was a sealed envelope labeled "Marc" in bold, black ink. My throat tightened as I tore it open.

Inside the envelope were photographs printed in a glossy finish. Each frame was crystal clear with no hazy pixel in sight.

There was one of me jamming a body into the dish cart, the bald forehead of the victim poking out of the cabinet.

There was another candid shot of me pushing the cart through the hall. There were more than just photos of me at the restaurant. There were shots of me walking around the neighborhood. Pictures of my ex-wife and her daughter at the mall. Photos of my mother and father watching television in their home, their bodies comfortably lounging on their sofa.

My heart beat at a dangerous pace as I flipped through the stacks of photos. Something else was jammed into the bottom corner of the envelope. When I pulled it out, I gasped. It was the crinkled paper note I had written to Julie. In my messy handwriting, it read:

There are bodies in the carts. Call 9-11.

In utter shock, I dropped the contents of the envelope. The photos scattered across the concrete, floating away in the wind. I dropped to my knees, rapidly stuffing the contents back inside. Some of the photos were traveling toward my neighbor's lawn in a carefree gust of wind. I scurried across the drive pad to collect them, glancing up at the sleepy suburban neighborhood, the place I had called home for decades. It suddenly didn't feel so homely.

One of the photos that was carried across the lawn had flipped over.

There was writing in permanent marker on the back:
Welcome to the family.

Part 3: The Neighbor

The comfort of my home did little to calm my nerves.

The doors were locked, but the damage had been done.

Silva was watching. He'd been watching for God knows how long, tracking me and my closest loved ones in order to ensure everything was kept in the "family". The photos were a clever insurance policy—a weapon to wield if things went south. Now I was stuck under his thumb with my real family within his crosshairs.

What a difference a day could make. Not even twenty-four hours ago, I was just a lowly server. Now I was sitting in the dark, trawling through the shady corners of the internet. Hunched over my laptop in my pajamas, I scrolled through the various internet tabs, each one more incriminating than the next:

Where do you buy a burner phone?

How do you know you're being stalked?

How much jail time for the possession of a dead body?

Maybe the police would believe my story. Maybe if I showed them where the bodies were, maybe if I could get my hands on the security footage, this could all end. I could go back to living a normal life.

But maybe they wouldn't.

And who was I kidding? Life was never going to return to normal. For the brief moments when I managed to doze off, all I saw were their cloudy eyes. The victims will never let me sleep. Every shadowy corner was a threat concealing one of Silva's henchmen; every creak from the floorboards made me jolt. Nothing felt safe as the night crawled on.

It wasn't until a hint of amber broke through a gray arc of cloud that the harsh reality set in: I wasn't going to figure this out alone. I needed to talk to someone, someone I trusted to keep quiet. Someone who had information that I didn't. Someone hiding a secret as dark as my own.

Someone I think I loved, as fucked up as that was.

It was an impossible thing to explain. The cold hard facts were there: I stared into her husband's lifeless eyes, and I carried out her children's limp bodies. And yet, here I was, still in love. I just couldn't shake it. The Paulina I knew was warm, inviting, and full of heart. I had known that woman for years. Despite my apprehension surrounding that evening, I still held out hope that there was something I didn't fully understand.

When the sun rose and the songbirds chirped their familiar chorus, I rose from under the heaps of blankets and ran a hot shower. After breakfast, I made my way to Paulina's house. The usual characters were moseying around outside: Joe from across the street was firing up his lawnmower, the purr from the engine overtaking the birds' tunes. Debbie was strolling around her front yard with her little cockapoo on leash. I only made it a few steps past my driveway before I noticed that she had company—parked beside the red minivan was an empty squad car.

Shit.

I darted toward Debbie, the self-proclaimed "eclectic" neighbor on our block. We stood on the sidewalk outside of her aquamarine-painted home, the rainbow pinwheel lawn ornaments stabbed into her lawn at seemingly random locations. I dove into some polite conversation, all the while keeping my attention on Paulina's home. Ten minutes of chit-chat went by with no movement from her residence.

"Any idea what's going on at Paulina's?" I casually asked.

"No idea," a hint of a smirk emerging on her face. She couldn't resist the delectable piece of gossip. "You know," Debbie said, her voice now an excited whisper, "I think there's some trouble in paradise..."

"What do you mean by that?" I pried. Debbie was basically our neighborhood watch. At her age, there wasn't much else for her to do.

"Oh," she remarked, "I always knew that Keith was trouble. Coming home at all hours of the night with that obnoxiously loud exhaust." She tugged on Romeo's leash, his nose deep in a pile of his own droppings. "I've seen him with another gal, you know. A dark-haired girl. Trashy little thing with tattoos."

This was all news to me. I paused to take it all in, petting Romeo on his head. "That is awful, really awful. But that's far from a crime, Debbie."

"You know, I wouldn't be surprised if he hit her."

"Debbie..." I groaned.

She doubled down. "He's got a temper on him, that's all. I've seen him toss rocks at poor Romeo when he was barking. He thought I wasn't looking, but I was."

My stomach churned knowing we were speaking ill about someone who was murdered. While Debbie continued rambling on about other neighbors' deplorable acts, out of the corner of my eye I saw two cops walk out of Paulina's house.

"I've got to grab the mail, Deb. Nice chatting with you." I waved goodbye as the squad car cruised out of the cul-de-sac.

I waited outside of Moody's Backroom, underneath the humming neon sign. I wondered if I was making a big mistake.

A murderer and her accomplice enter a bar.

It all feels like one bad joke, and something tells me I won't be around to hear the punch line.

Moody's Backroom is not like Azalea's. It's a roof and four walls with a couple of rusty kegs. It's got a flashing neon sign that you could spot from outer space. There are signs promoting their daily food and drink specials on every street corner in the neighborhood. This is a place begging for service, *anybody's* service.

How I got here is still a whirlwind. On Saturday, I retreated back to my house and opted to stay in. I figured Paulina had too much heat on her to risk any interaction. I was out of luck and out of time. But as fate would have it, Paulina spotted me on Sunday on my way back from a morning jog. I was hoping the endorphins would help clear my head, but all they did was leave me exhausted. I couldn't resist her wave, and in a split second, I found myself standing on her porch. She had a strawberry lemonade in hand and a smile across her face. Her hair sparkled in the sunlight; she looked radiant given the circumstances. We chatted for a bit as I tussled with my attraction to her and the reality of our situation. She extended another offer to grab a drink, and in a sudden, helpless reflex, I said yes. The brain seemed to be no match for the heart.

Once she arrived she gave me a hug, and we grabbed seats in plain view of the VLT's. We people-watched for a while, chatting about the weather and the news. We discussed her vacation plans to Mexico and her current projects at work. Our first round was casual like this, like an awkward first date. Paulina's hair was in a messy bun, but her appearance was far from disheveled. She wore a boat neck sweater, silver hoop earrings, and a pair of Levi's jeans. It was what I imagined a night out with her to be like. This was the Paulina that I knew.

Two rounds in, and the conversation started to get more personal. Paulina asked me about my history, so I told her about my divorce and how my dating life has been. I had her full attention; I could see the interest in her eyes. I really didn't know what else to ask her at this point, so I just kept going on about myself.

Three drinks in, and the alcohol had washed away all of the nervous energy. We were floating through conversation with light-hearted, friendly banter. She playfully patted my arm, and my instincts took over. I knew it was time to chip away at her fortress of secrets. The liquid courage was flowing foolishly through me now, so I began to ask the bold questions, the questions I had been dying to ask all night.

"How are you doing, Paulina?"

She looked puzzled, as she sipped her Mai Tai through a straw. "What's wrong with you?" she joked. " I'm doing good... how about you?"

I leaned in, my voice falling to a gentle whisper. "No, I mean, how are you *really* doing?"

She placed her drink down and cocked her head to the side.

"It can't be easy."

"Beg your pardon?"

I sighed, leaning closer. In a low voice, I asked her how her family is doing.

She paused, stirring her drink. "Oh, they're doing well," she said. "That does remind me though, I should check in with Keith." She pulled out her cell phone and just as she held it to her ear, I placed my hand on her arm.

"Paulina. I know."

She squinted.

"Yesterday, at the restaurant. The cop car this morning."

I saw the color slowly drain from her face. Her eyes moistened, glistening under the pendant light above us. For a moment, there was a pause that felt like the whole world was waiting.

"I don't know what you're talking about," she said, sinking in her seat. The shift in energy was now palpable; the room felt cold, and I could feel her slowly pull away.

"I'm sorry. It's too soon..." I sighed. "I just... I thought... I just really need to know."

One quick glance at the exit, and she proceeded to grab her purse. "Wait, Paulina," I begged. "Hear me out for a second. Please."

"There's nothing to know," she declared. She stood up. I followed suit, reaching for her shoulder.

"Paulina," I shouted. "I won't tell anybody. I swear."

The bell above the exit door jingled as it swung shut behind her.

⬡

After paying the tab, I drove home, knowing that I shouldn't. I was tiptoeing the line of sobriety with an empty stomach. The hard liquor and dark thoughts swirled around inside of me in a noxious concoction. I screamed, pounding the wheel.

You fuck up.

You idiot.

It was a short route home through residential streets. The cookie-cutter homes were mere blurs of color as I drove past. Besides the parked cars, the roads were empty, the sidewalks bare.

In my rearview, I noticed a black SUV behind me. It turned left when I turned left. I thought I was overreacting; so I tested my theory and took another left into a nearby cul-de-sac. The vehicle followed me in a loop past the row of two-story homes. My chest began to tighten. My only thought was that I can't go home. So I kept driving down Citadel road. Citadel Crescent. Citadel Circle. Leaving the community, I headed down Mckenzie boulevard with the SUV on my tail.

Eventually, I knew I would have to stop. I just didn't know where to go. My heart beat so violently that I could feel it pulsating in my skull. I figured the safest place was somewhere public, so I decided to pull into the Southside strip mall. The grocery store parking lot wasn't exactly packed: there were some scattered RVs and late-night shoppers, but otherwise it was empty.

I parked near a row of cars and waited. The SUV pulled up right beside me. The tint on the passenger-side window was too opaque to see through; I could only hear the opening and then slamming of the driver-side door.

"Get out of the car," the voice commanded.

The glow from the lamp post revealed a curly-haired woman. Both of her arms were crossed and covered in an elaborate sleeve of tattoos: two colorful intersecting gardens of fully bloomed flowers in an elaborate water-mark style.

I rolled down the window a fraction of an inch and yelled back, "Why are you following me you psycho?"

"Who the hell are you? And what are you doing with Paulina?"

I rolled down the window a little more and noticed the distinct characteristics of her face: dark brown hair and ice-blue eyes. Her prominent nose. Her tall stature. She was sitting at the table next to ours, and up close she looked incredibly familiar. The resemblance was uncanny.

"Calm down for a second," I said, stepping out of my vehicle. "No reason to get all worked up. We are just friends."

"Bullshit," she hissed. "*You* know something. I can feel it."

By now, a small crowd of shoppers were enjoying the show, their hands gripping plastic bags full of groceries, their carts abandoned on the side of the road.

With a sudden eruption, the dark-haired woman that could only be Keith's sister shouted back to the crowd:

"I'm calling the cops. This man's a murderer."

Part 4: The Last Supper

The crowd feasted their eyes on the drama ensuing. The woman who I believed to be Keith's sister had a fiery look in her eyes. I felt horrible for her family, but she was looking for answers to questions that I just couldn't provide. Silva had me backed into a corner with jail time or collateral damage as the only ways out.

"Can we relax for a second?" I pleaded. "I'm just the neighbor—Marc. That's it."

"Well you two sure look like cozy neighbors," she scoffed. Her hands were shaking as she held her phone to her ear.

"Stop for a Goddamn second!" I yelled. There was a gasp from someone in the crowd. The woman resembling Keith nearly dropped her phone. "Call the cops, then. Go on. Is going to the bar a crime? You'll do nothing but look crazy."

The woman glared back, eventually taking the phone from her ear. She placed it in her palm, squeezing it violently as she screeched. I took a step back, as did some of the closer shoppers.

"You two did something to him," she declared, tears welling up in her eyes. "I know it." She pointed her finger at me, her body trembling, "And if you're stupid enough to be with her, she will do the same to you."

There was silence for a moment as the woman paced around the lot. She eventually broke down and began to sob as she found a seat on the curb, her face shielded by her hands. The crowd slowly dispersed. Once she calmed down, we were able to make a proper introduction. Her name was Viola, and she confirmed that she was Keith's baby sister. Keith was her only sibling, and she became concerned when he hadn't responded to her text messages Friday evening. When he no-showed for their brunch plans

Saturday morning, that's when she really began to worry. Paulina had recently decided that the family was going to move out of the country with little warning or consultation provided to Keith. This was how Paulina was—the qualities that made her fun were also what made her dangerous. Keith had become fed up with her unpredictable nature, and the extended family was worried that with the move they would never see their children again.

All I could offer were some hollow words of encouragement: remain calm and hope for the best. I could tell they did little to soothe her. We eventually said goodbye, the lies tossing around in the pit of my stomach knowing that her brother was never coming home.

With one bomb carefully diffused, I went home to think through the major issue at hand. My plan to build a closer relationship with Paulina had gone up in flames. There was no new information garnered; the opportunity had been wasted. I suffered one more sleepless night, and before I knew it, the weekend was over.

In the morning, I peeked out my window. Paulina's driveway was empty. On my way to work, I saw Viola walking down the street with a small gathering of people. They were maybe three blocks from my house. In her hand was a stack of papers. At one of the nearby light posts, I pulled over to look at what they were taping to the metal structures:

HELP BRING KEITH BARGALLO HOME.

Keith Bargallo: a loving husband, devoted father, and up-standing member of our community has been missing since Friday, April 30th. There is a cash reward for anyone who can provide information on his whereabouts or the whereabouts of his wife, Paulina, and their two children, Riley and Colton.

Help us bring him home.

A phone number was highlighted at the bottom of the page. The photo on the flyer was a family portrait taken at a nearby park.

Jesus, that was quick, I thought. The dust had barely settled, and Viola was already sniffing around, as a good sister would. I gripped the wheel, the photo of their happy family haunting me all the way to the restaurant.

There was the usual rush of workers at Azalea's. They were scuttling through the halls, heading to the nearby change rooms, and preparing the tables for the upcoming dinner service. As I left the front of the house towards the changing room, I caught a glimpse of Silva. He was walking at a brisk pace down the hall with a couple of other associates. It was only a quick flash of his black and silver crewcut, it was only the back of his head, but that's all it took to make me suddenly feel a chill run up my neck.

Dewayne was dawdling around by his locker with a couple of the other cooks when I entered.

"You have a good weekend, Marc?" he grinned. "Ready for some more training? This time, I won't go easy."

"Sorry, Dewayne," I said, while removing my shoes. "I told you that bussing ain't for me. I'm back to serving today."

"Well, that's news to me," he shrugged. "Silva told me I was training you again this evening."

"Well, he must have forgotten," I grumbled, buttoning my shirt. "I discussed this with him on Friday."

Dewayne's face was blank, apathetic. He fiddled with something in his pocket. "Either way, it don't matter to me. Just let me know what he says before the rush starts." He playfully swatted one of the cooks in the belly before leaving. "Let's go get that money, boys!"

I stared blankly at the lockers as flashbacks of Friday flooded my brain: the contorted bodies stuffed in the dish cart, the squishing of bloated flesh, the cracking of bones. There was no way in hell

I was ever going back to bussing. Silva and I would need to have another word.

After I changed into my uniform, I went to help set the tables and fold some last-minute cutlery. I hoped to cross paths with Silva; he was usually running up and down the halls leading up to service, but tonight I wasn't so lucky. His office door was locked and my knocking went unanswered.

Lana waved at me from down the hall. I had already seen Greg at the lockers and passed by Steph and Kelly wrapping cutlery. By my count, we were already fully staffed for servers, and that number excluded me.

With twenty minutes to go before service, I began to panic. I asked Mia, the hostess, if she had seen Silva around.

"Sorry, haven't seen him."

"Does he have any appointments?" I asked, scratching my head.

She scrolled through the tablet and confirmed he didn't. As I approached the hostess podium, I noticed something resting on one of the shelves behind it. It was a cellphone with a glittery phone case and a distinct Hello-Kitty tassel wrapped around the headphone jack opening.

"Julie working tonight?" I asked.

"No. Just me," she sighed. "Worked all weekend, too. So freakin' sick of this place..."

I pointed to the phone behind the podium.

"Oh, my God. Wow. Didn't even notice that! She must have been going nuts all weekend."

Before Mia could continue, Lana approached and asked her a question about the menu. The server whisked her away toward one of the dining rooms in order to investigate the error. Before she left, Mia patted me on the shoulder, "I'll stop by her place tonight and drop it off. Thanks, Marc."

A wary smile grew on my face.

Once they were out of sight, I began to snoop around the podium. On the bottom shelf there was a black purse. It had a matching tassel. The stupid cat seemed to be waving at me from the ground.

I froze. Her wallet, her keys—everything was still in the bag.

The memory of the note began to resurface and suddenly my limbs felt weak. I jumped to the only logical conclusion:

Julie never left.

I wandered down the halls, rummaging through the storage rooms in the kitchen and the dish room. I opened any door I walked past, searching for signs of Julie. My heart beat aggressively in my chest with every failed attempt. There was no doubt that Dewayne was looking for me too; my watch told me that the dinner crowd would be arriving any minute...

A cold hand grabbed my shoulder from behind. The sudden movement made me flinch.

"Geez, Marc. Relax," Lana laughed. "Tell everyone you see to come down to room one. They're gathering everyone together for a meeting."

"What's going on?" I asked.

Monday nights were always our slowest, but the complete absence of foot traffic was very concerning. I followed her down the empty hallway.

"I don't know. Silva told me to sweep the halls to find any stragglers. I think you're the last one."

When we arrived, a burly, bald man held the door open for us. He was a familiar face, someone I seldom saw this deep inside the restaurant. He wasn't an employee as far as I could tell, just some sort of supplier I'd see around the kitchen from time to time.

The air was thick. You could feel the heat radiating off the walls the moment you entered; there were far too many people for the tight space. Employees seated across the long table looked nervously around the room. Those that weren't early enough to nab seats were standing in a line along the walls. On top of the table were beautiful arrays of mouth-watering appetizers: bacon-wrapped prunes, blini with caviar, beef tartare, and cheese fondue. A strange man with squinty eyes was pouring shots of alcohol out of mini liquor bottles, while the bald man from the doorway followed him toward the table holding a bottle of wine. They passed around glasses to everyone.

"Wine or liqueur?" the squinty man asked. Through pursed lips, I replied, "I'm okay."

"Wine or liqueur?" he repeated. "*Come on*, we're celebrating!"

I hesitated, eyeing the room. Eventually, I pointed to the bottle of red.

The bald man poured a generous amount and handed me the glass.

"Is this everyone?" he asked the room. A couple of people nodded their heads in assurance.

"Okay," the squinty man shouted. "Well, first off, I'd like to introduce myself. My name is Sergio. I'm one of the main investors in Azalea's."

Lana and myself shared puzzled looks. I had never seen this man before.

"The success of this restaurant has not been lost on myself or any of the other investors. We are incredibly proud of what this restaurant has accomplished, and that starts with each and every one of you." He raised a glass. "I propose a toast: to the staff that makes this place special—from the cooking staff to the servers, the hostesses to the busboys. You are all an integral part of this family, and we need to do much more in terms of showing you our gratitude."

While Sergio spoke, I scanned the room. There was still no sign of Julie, or better yet, no sign of Silva. I clinked my glass against Lana's and a few other employees in my vicinity, holding the brim of the glass to my lips. Some of the wait staff had downed their drinks and were nibbling at the finger food. Some of the line cooks and junior chefs were pouring themselves another round with delighted smiles across their faces. This was the first teambuilding event in all my years at the restaurant, so many of the workers seemed to be making the most out of the occasion. But those that knew better held their ground. Dewayne held his full glass to his hip with a stern expression. Elsa was sitting at the table, her chef hat flopping out of her pocket, her glass untouched. I had seen too much death to enjoy the festivities.

"You should try the tartare," Lana whispered. "It's delicious."

I smiled, wine glass still to my mouth, as I eyed the exit. I slowly shuffled toward the door as the speech continued.

"Tonight—we celebrate our employees. Dinner service has been canceled. And don't worry, taxi services will be provided to those who will need it."

The roar from the room was deafening.

"Before we start the festivities, there is one more exciting announcement."

The door slowly creaked open, the sound lost amongst the celebration. "We will be reopening at a new location. A much bigger venue." The excitement slowly shifted into nervous apprehension. "Do not worry," Sergio assured the crowd. "You will all be welcomed back with open arms. Azalea's needs each and every one of you. Now, more than ever!"

The dim light sparkled off the chandeliers in an eyrie dance as I strolled through the halls. I walked past the foyer into the kitchen, and then down the grungy, abandoned hallway. With everyone preoccupied with the party, it gave me an opportunity to go digging for some answers. As I made it closer to the elevator, I detected movement. My walk turned into a run as I saw Martin's lanky figure. The door to the elevator was slowly closing.

I pounded my feet into the concrete and sprinted as fast as I could. With an outstretched hand, I managed to activate the sensor just as the door was closing.

"What the fuck are you doing?" he barked.

I grabbed him by his scrawny neck and pinned him to the back of the elevator. "Take me down. Now."

He flailed and sent a powerful kick to my stomach. I noticed his hands were coated in a thick layer of blood. Wheezing and clutching my midriff, I yelled, "Take me to the bodies, you piece of shit!"

We grappled with each other, spilling into the hallway. He managed to clip me on the side of the head with a shot that made me wobble. With gritted teeth, we both struggled for control. I wrestled with him, holding his body close to mine as I tried to recover. The dim light from the elevator was sparking like little flashes of lightning. The room spun dangerously, but somehow with a sudden burst of energy, I managed to connect with a short jab. It stunned Martin long enough for me to push him into the wall. He went flying, his head hitting the corner of the exposed brick. There was a deep thud before his body collapsed to the floor. A small trail of blood trickled out of the side of his skull. It began to form a tiny puddle on the floor.

I scrambled to his body, rummaging for his access key. There were sounds coming out of me that I'd never heard before. Uncontrollable sobs. Moans of sorrow. I found the card in his back pocket and booked it for the elevator. As the doors began to close, I noticed the blinking red light coming from the ceiling. The camera stared back in my direction.

The odor was crippling, it crept up the shaft and seeped through the cracks of the elevator doors. The elevator carriage rumbled as I slowly descended into the unknown. The doors slid open to reveal what looked like an ongoing construction project. The framing and some of the drywall had been completed, but the floor largely consisted of packed dirt, and darkness seemed to cover large sections of the room. There were lights strung up on the ceiling, but there was little done to mask the smell. If there wasn't a pile of gas masks laid out by the entrance, I surely would have vomited.

I followed the hanging, glowing orbs down the tunnel. It only took a couple of paces before I saw the industrial-sized fridge. It was a massive stainless-steel house with a large sliding door. I shivered as I entered the unit. Inside were shelves and shelves of plastic bags:

Hearts, livers, lungs, intestines, and vials of blood.

Names of either the victims or the new recipients were written in permanent marker. Everything was sealed, labeled, and organized. I tiptoed deeper into the cool room, only making it a few more steps before I finally screamed.

Silva was rigid and face-up, lying on top of a pile of bodies. Thousand-dollar suits and flowing gowns were all lined with speckles of frost. Silva's eyebrows were covered in an icy white, his expression frozen in a look of terror. The bullet wound was right through the center of his head.

At that moment, I understood that this was more than a murder-for-hire operation. It was so much more than a restaurant. Everything seemed to turn a profit.

I ran out of the frigid room and started pacing outside of the unit. I wanted so badly to go back up the elevator, to make my way to safety. But I knew I was on the cusp of uncovering the secrets; there was still so much I didn't know potentially down the hall. So I foolishly pressed forward.

As I stepped further and further into the basement, the smell intensified. The piles of bodies were in plain sight—if you could even call them bodies anymore.

I removed my mask, just in time to unleash a violent wave of chicken casserole.

Their stomachs were fleshy, gaping holes, hacked away with little left of their insides except for the rib cages and bone that held the remaining bits of skin together. Their faces had no eyes, just black holes carved out of the now rotting flesh. The maggots were little white dots in a sea of decomposed skin, festering all through the crevices of what was left. The dirt floor had clearly been disturbed in numerous places.

Jesus.

Christ.

Something drew me toward one of the hands dangling from the middle of the pile. It was dainty, the fingernails painted in a pastel pumpkin. The flamboyant color palette looked familiar, like something Julie would wear. As I pulled, heaps of limbs and serrated bones toppled from the top of the tower of bodies. Roves of beetles and blowflies buzzed from all of the commotion.

I recoiled, losing my footing on some loose sediment.

In the corner of my eye, I spotted the meat grinder at the end of the room. The piece of machinery was hiding in the shadows, kept from plain sight. As I got closer, I could see that the thing looked polished to perfection. Sinister thoughts flooded my brain regarding its purpose.

Some off-menu items for an extra cost? A special order of beef tartare? The chunks of meat caught on the blades looked fresh. I dry-heaved, nearly losing my lunch once again.

These were all of Azalea's deepest, darkest secrets. Secrets that some of the family members took to the grave.

I needed to leave before I suffered the same fate.

There was a thundering sound of footsteps and scraping coming from the ceiling. I made a mad dash for the elevator. I strode past Martin's body and made it through the empty kitchen. I managed to round the corner of the foyer before I heard shouting:

"Hey, you! Stop!"

The bald man was wheeling one of the dish carts out of room one. Dewayne was wheeling another behind him.

I took flight up the stairs, hearing the pounding of ominous footsteps behind me. I managed to exit the parking lot before they were able to get close.

I told you at the start of all of this that I was a nobody. I was just a lowly server. I was no mastermind. I was no criminal, despite what the security tapes may have shown.

There was no plan. There was nothing.

There was no gun. Although, I did think about this often during my fits of insomnia. I would have been too much of a coward to ever pull the trigger. But if anyone deserved a bullet to their brain, it was Silva. It would have been satisfying to do the honor, but the end result was the same.

There was no fake passport. I just couldn't figure out where to find one.

There was no burner phone. I never had the gumption to follow through.

In the end, there was just me and the open road.

My first stop was a small-town bank in the early morning. I withdrew all the cash that I could and loaded it into a suitcase. I kept driving, only stopping to load up on fuel or to reload on convenience store snacks and energy drinks. I kept going for a few days until I reached the Mexican border. I prayed they would let me through, and for some reason, my prayers were answered. The Azalea family always proved to be a tight-lipped bunch.

There exists a beach along the coast just outside of a small town. I remembered the recommendation from a dear friend. It was off the beaten path and far away from tourists. I think the name was El Desembo. Or maybe Desemboke? My Spanish was never the greatest, it just seemed like a good place to stop.

The crystal-clear water shimmered as the tide rolled in and out. I was just in time for the sunset. There were some Mexican teenagers splashing around in the water and a handful of fishermen dragging around empty nets across the beach. Apart from that, it was peaceful.

There was one other person on the beach, the only other gringo that I'd seen in a while. Her hair was an unusual midnight black for her fair complexion. Her smile glimmered in a familiar way. She looked alone and out of place, but despite it all, she looked happy. Gazing at her sprawled out on her beach towel, I suddenly felt the need to make a call.

I dialed the number, the same one from the poster.

"Hello?"

"Viola?"

"Yes. And who is this?"

"It was her," I said. "You were right all along." And I told her everything.

❖

The sun dipped below the horizon, the sky gradually turning a murky marmalade. It was harder and harder to see with every passing second.

My mind wandered into the dark recesses of my brain, towards the memories I tried to forget. I reflected on my time at Azalea's and how great the job truly was, before it wasn't. I thought about my coworkers. I thought about Julie. I thought about how close I came to death. I thought about the others who weren't so lucky. I thought about the life I took and the one that got away.

The beach was empty now: the fishing boats all secured and hitched to the dock for the evening. My vision was hazy in the shadows, but I still heard the playful frolicking in the water and the soothing splash of the waves against the rocks.

At that moment, I was sure—this was the most beautiful place in the world.

I figured it was only a matter of time before they found me. Whether they tracked my cell signal from the nearby towers or found the footage from the restaurant. Tomorrow, I will be in another town, and another after that, for as long and as far as my money will take me.

But for now, I sat and took in the crashing of the waves. Awaiting the dead, restless eyes that would undoubtedly come for me in my sleep.

THE KALEIDOSCOPE

Here she was, again. Waiting.

From twenty stories up, the people looked like ants to Cora. Hundreds of them scurrying up and down the pavement, all with their own agendas and places to be. Cora's place was here—and it had taken two buses and one long sprint that tested the soles of her sneakers—but she had made it, all the same. Out of breath, but just in time for her appointment. She stared out the window of the Jamison towers office suite and admired the hazy glow of the streetlights.

The chalk-white walls of the office looked identical to the others. Professional, neat, and clean. There was a dreary hum and a light breeze of recirculated air blowing in from the vents.

She was alone, fanning through the assortment of magazines on the table before opting for one of the National Geographics. Elevator music played gently in the background. As she settled in, her eyes glanced down the row of plaques mounted on the wall. The frames showcased all of Dr. Holloway's various certificates and diplomas.

The doctor was clearly qualified. On paper, they all were.

It was easy to find help (being able to afford it was another matter), but she never had a problem locating some schlub with a fancy degree that could write up a prescription. If it was just a matter of numbing out, Cora could have just taken the pills and saved herself the rigamarole.

But *good* help was hard to come by. And Dr. Holloway was supposedly the best.

So, she waited. The clock above the door ticked and ticked.

When he finally arrived, the first thing she noticed was his height. A distinguished tower of a man entered the room, his glossy horn-rimmed glasses as black as a starless night.

He cleared his throat. "Mrs. Searcy?" He stuck out his hand and they shook.

"Hello."

"I'm Dr. Holloway. It's a pleasure to finally meet you."

Cora flashed him a coy smile.

He walked over to the window and waved for her to follow. Dr. Holloway sunk into the leather chair and Cora took the sofa across from him. She nearly stumbled into the lamp that looped over the coffee table between them. The glow from the nearby apartment buildings lit up the night sky.

His dark walnut eyes stared into hers. "So, Cora. How can I help you?"

She shifted her gaze to the window and the lights of the big city. The beginning was always the most awkward. "I... yes. I'm hoping you can help me out. Where would you like me to start?"

"From the beginning, please," he said. "From the first time you heard the voices."

She fidgeted in her seat. "*The voices?*"

Dr. Holloway's smile had vanished as he grabbed his notebook from the coffee table. He wedged it into the corner of the seat before speaking again. "Cora, I want to help you. I do. But let's not beat around the bush here. It's smoother when all the cards are on the table, don't you think? Makes my job a whole lot easier." He pulled out a cloth from his shirt pocket and began to wipe his glasses. "What do you say?"

Cora hesitated. "I think you may have me confused with some-one else?"

He blew a heavy sigh. They both sat in silence for a moment, staring out the window.

The doctor rubbed his forehead before leaning back in his chair. "I guess so," he concluded. He grabbed the notebook and flipped through the pages, stopping eventually at a blank page. "My apologies, Cora," he said, a smile returning to his face. "Please continue."

Weird, she thought. *Very weird.*

"Well, I've been having some dark thoughts lately. And I guess... I just don't know who to turn to."

"What sort of thoughts?"

The words crawled out cautiously from Cora's mouth, "Thoughts of... ending my life."

Dr. Holloway contorted his lips. His response was more of a grunt: "*Hmmm.*" He jotted something down before speaking. "I'm so sorry to hear that, Cora. How long have you been having these troublesome thoughts?"

"Off and on, ever since I was a little girl. But it seems lately they've been escalating. And it's never been as bad as it's been these past few months."

"And these thoughts—can you please elaborate?"

"When I was younger, it was a lot of negative self-chatter. Regrets really about my... how do I put this? My less-than-perfect moments. Just times when I was selfish or deceitful or whatever. I used to really stew about those things. I used to really hate myself." She sighed. "But it's gotten to this point where everything feels pointless. I feel worthless. And the nightmares, Doc. I've been waking up in cold sweats..."

Dr. Holloway tapped the pen he was holding against his thigh. "I see, I see. Okay. A lot to unpack here." He continued, his head down, vehemently scribbling down notes. "Can you start with the nightmares?"

Cora glanced up at the clock. She understood that as a first-time patient, a therapist would require some background information, some history, before he could properly assess the situation and recommend treatment. But this wasn't going as expected. He was supposed to be *different*. And this session felt like any of the other dozens of appointments she had been to over the course of her life. She had been psycho-analyzed enough to know the chain of events that would follow: she would go into heavy detail about the nightmares which would soak up most of the time, and then the doctor would inquire about her medical history. Then she would be sent home with a piece of paper written in chicken scratch. It would be a prescription for either the pink pills, the orange pills, or the green ones. She had sampled the whole damn rainbow, it didn't matter. They would be just enough to tie her over until the next appointment.

And then the next one. And the next.

She was sick of the brain fog and the myriad of other side effects that came with the medication. None of it worked. So, she decided that this would be her last appointment. There was a pile of rope in her closet, waiting. If Dr. Holloway was so exceptional, he would have one shot, the final kick of the can, to save her.

After Cora described her nightmares and rattled off her medication history, Dr. Holloway finished writing a few more notes before placing the book on the table. The hour was nearly up.

"Thank you, Cora. I think I have everything that I need." He got up and patted the cushioned head of the sofa she was seated on. "Please—lie down for a moment."

She followed his instructions. Cora watched him walk over to his desk and rummage through one of the drawers.

"Please relax. Close your eyes."

Cora took another look at the clock and swallowed. They were just past an hour, and at her grocery clerk's salary, she was scared she couldn't cover the additional charge.

"Please, don't worry," he assured her. "We are almost done."

She shut her eyes, and the room went dark. The sound of footsteps approached from behind her.

"Now I need you to trust me here. This is something that I try with all my clients."

She felt a strap tighten around the back of her head. There was sudden pressure around her left eye. Around her right eye, she felt a sweaty palm. She began to squirm.

"Relax. Please keep your eyes closed."

Her heart was racing, but she obeyed.

"Now, this is a bit unconventional, but I find this method really helps my clients loosen up. It will feel weird at first, but please remain calm."

Cora felt a wave of radiating heat. She imagined the lamp directly over her. *Why did he need the light?*

"Okay. I want you to open just your left eye, please. When I say so."

The room went quiet, except for his heavy breathing. She felt his hand grasp hers.

"Okay. Take a deep breath. And when I say open, you feel this dial? Turn it and open your eye. You understand?"

Cora nodded nervously.

"Okay. And—open."

She turned the dial, and what she saw were patterns of immeasurable color. Deep bursts of sapphire blue transformed into waves of bright cyan. The different hues sparkled together in a mesmerizing dance. Twirling shamrock green rhombuses flipped and spun along her plane of vision, eventually morphing into streaks of electric pink. The layers of shades seemed to span the entire spectrum. With every second, the colors spread across her line of sight before eventually being swallowed up by a thin border of black. The captivating display was both dizzying and alluring.

"What do you see?" the doctor asked.

Cora murmured, "Colors. Beautiful colors." She noticed a trickle of drool running down the corner of her mouth.

"Good," Dr. Holloway replied. His voice fell to a whisper, "Now clear your mind, and focus on your breathing."

There was a sharp pain around her left eye as the pressure intensified.

Her chest rose and fell like a wave.

Inhale.

Exhale.

The colors morphed, twisting and twirling, exploding with the intensity of fireworks only for the vibrance to fizzle away in a matter of seconds. She noticed she was no longer spinning the dial; she no longer felt a hand shielding her right eye.

"Good, Cora. Good."

The colors were taking on shapes and patterns that Cora had never seen before. She didn't know what to make of the strange sensation, but she lay there, body quivering, as a tear trickled down her cheek.

"Let go, Cora. Let go."

Her heart beat feverishly. In a swirl of indigo and turquoise, just before the colors disappeared, she saw something expand. It was an orb absent of color that didn't move like the other shapes. Through the splashes of color, it approached, splitting into two and diverting into opposite corners.

The orbs swelled and pulsated in their place, never rotating, never pin-wheeling off to be swallowed up by another color. They were constant. And once Cora spotted the flicker, she was sure of what she saw.

The orbs were blinking.

They leered back at Cora, a menacing gaze that was only broken by the occasional shape that floated past.

Cora let out a scream that shook the room.

"Relax, my dear. This is all part of the process. Take another deep breath and just listen."

She attempted to break free, but something heavy held her in place. She imagined the silhouette of Dr. Holloway straddling her.

"You're not listening!" he barked.

She shrieked again, pleading for help. A low rumble cut her off, the voice almost animalistic.

Greed.

Greed.

Greed.

"You've spent your whole life trying to keep them out. Why not try to let the voices in?"

Her right eye, previously covered in darkness, became illuminated with the scenes from her nightmares. The visions played as she helplessly looked on. Cora saw herself take a knife to her throat, slicing the veins and cartilage open with a single, fatal swipe. The blood spilled out of the wound, running down her pale neck before her body finally collapsed.

Another cry screeched from her throat as she felt the searing pain around her neck. She touched the wound in disbelief.

Dr. Holloway continued to whisper in her ear, but her focus was on the next scene. This time she was clutching a Smith & Wesson. All her research had told her that it would be painless, that a bullet to the brain was one of the easiest paths to leave the world behind.

It wasn't.

Lies.

Lies.

Lies.

The voice growled from the sea of fragmented colors. Something prevented her from looking away; a force wedged her eyelids open.

Next was a bottle of Vicodin, followed by a plunge into the pavement from the roof of her ten-story apartment building.

The whole time, Dr. Holloway cooly purred instructions. As she watched herself lying in the murky waters of her yellowed bathtub, Cora finally listened.

"You don't have to suffer like this anymore. There is a way out. You can be free."

Her lungs burned like they had been barbecued. She watched the saddest version of herself floating lifelessly in the water.

"Just let the voices in, for once. Listen—*truly* listen. And if you decide yes, then let go."

Cora realized that these were the voices all along: telling her that she wasn't good enough, telling her that she was worthless. It wasn't her voice, it was *theirs*.

The black orbs drifted toward the middle of the light show. They began to multiply and gravitate closer together. She now stared at the cluster of beady red eyes that steadily approached.

"Let go," Dr. Holloway whispered.

And whether it was the exhaustion of suffering repeated deaths or the overwhelming contrast between the beauty of the lights, Cora finally decided to let go.

The chant intensified like she was nose-to-nose with the beings.

She decided to finally listen.

Feed.

Feed.

Feed.

Die.

Die.

Die.

The hooded entities surrounded her.

Dazzling beams of dandelion yellow and sparkling fuchsia flared out of the shadows beneath their hoods. She collapsed as the souls siphoned her essence away.

"That's our time, Cora," Dr. Holloway said. "I'm so proud of the progress you have made. Look how far you've come."

Cora felt nothing as she let go, her eyes slowly closing shut.

She awoke, surrounded by a hundred shades of red. The pillars of light slowly phased into arcs of strawberry before deepening into a dark crimson. She sat up, alert. Huddled beside her were the hooded figures. It was difficult to differentiate the cloak from the being; the pigment of their skin was such a dense pool of black that it washed away any semblance of humanity.

The group paid Cora no mind; they seemed to be looking past her. When she turned around, she finally observed what had caught the attention of the crowd—a hazel sphere the size of a celestial body loomed before them. Its black center darted left and right among jagged, bloodshot-red constellations carved into a milky galaxy of white. Cora got up and stood with the others, in awe of the bulging brown sun. It was only a moment before it slipped away, for the last time, replaced by impenetrable shadows.

What was left of her was unknown. Her voice sounded soft, almost listless. She heard Dr. Holloway say something, but the sounds were only unintelligible murmurs echoed into the void.

What she heard distinctly was the ringtone coming from her phone. The sound that traveled into the void sounded distant and distorted like it was playing underwater, but the annoying jingle of chimes and bells was undeniable. Cora figured it was her mother checking in on her, and her heart sank.

There was a solid bang (the closing of a door? Or a drawer?) and the music was gone.

Cora thought she felt a faint breeze, but noticed it was a light brush of fabric that had been draped atop her head. The entity that had covered her with the garment drifted back toward the others. The cloak felt weightless—like a gown of feathers hugging her body. As she slipped her hands through the armholes, she noticed her olive complexion was slowly fading away. The color seeped out of her in wispy trails of light like sand escaping from a tiny crack in an hourglass. It was swallowed up by the vortex of swirling shapes and hues.

She felt depleted, but she also sensed that the brooding cloud of gloom that had followed her for her entire life, that heavy feeling of hopelessness, had somehow been lifted.

Had she been cured? Or trapped?

There were no voices now, only silence.

She pondered the separation from her body and what would happen to her physical self. It was too much for her to handle in her tired state of mind.

If she knew anything from her years of therapy, it was that you had to trust the process.

She had felt no pain. All she felt, deep down in the pit of her stomach, was an insatiable sense of hunger.

She stood with the others, admiring the colors.

Waiting.

OFF THE COAST OF NOWHERE

Mayday! Mayday!

The voice crackled through the speaker.

We have an emergency. Can anybody hear me?

Ben must have dozed off, but now he was wide awake.

"Air traffic control? Can you hear me?

His throat felt tight, constricted. He was at a loss for words.

I repeat, can anybody hear me? Our engine has failed. We are descending rapidly—15,000 feet and falling. Our coordinates are...

Suddenly a shriek of bloody murder raised the hairs upon his neck. He heard the puttering of a sickly motor, followed by another onslaught of screams.

Ben knew he had to do something, but he also knew he was no hero. Fear had this sudden way of creeping into his psyche, making his mind cloudy. He was already eyeing the exit. There was still time, he figured, but not much. If he was quick, he could pass it along—it could be someone else's problem, someone far more equipped to handle it.

A distinct cry for help stifled his cowardice escape. It was young, high-pitched. It could only have come from a child.

Please do something! Save us.

Get back! the pilot commanded. *Mr. Salvado, bring her back to her seat!*

It was the mention of the last name that lingered: *Salvado.* Why did it ring a bell?

There was a sudden explosion as the screams began to blur into one. A deep, hearty voice began reciting a prayer in Spanish.

It was then that Ben decided to speak:

"Hel... Hello?"

Hello? Air traffic control?

This is a dream, Ben told himself. It was the only explanation for the lunacy. Once he accepted this narrative, the words seemed to slide out of his throat.

"No. I'm... I'm just a boy."

You're what?

Moonlight peered into his bedroom through a tiny gap in the blinds. It illuminated the Marvel posters upon his walls: Captain America, Thor. They would have known what to do in this moment, but not Ben.

He sat up in his bed and repeated, "I'm just a boy!" He swallowed. "I think you have the wrong... um... station or something?"

The static continued, hissing out of the dusty speaker on his nightstand. He was surprised the radio was even functioning: the white paneling had browned, the wooden frame scuffed and warped. Still, he had snatched it from his grandfather's basement. It was meant as nothing more than a cool memento, but it had proven itself to be a trusty sleeping aid, until now.

The pilot barked an expletive.

Boy? Quickly write down our coordinates. Please! Send help as soon as you can.

"Okay," Ben responded. He rummaged through one of the drawers and found a pen. Scanning the room and out of options, he held out his palm. "I'm ready."

As the pilot spoke, Ben finally made the connection. It was his grandpa's favorite story to tell when he had one too many whiskeys.

The Salvado family was the wealthiest family in the Pacific Northwest. Their story had everything: romance, corruption, betrayal. He hadn't heard the tale in quite some time.

The best part about it was the mystery—the ending... or lack thereof.

8.8 degrees south... 122 degrees...

Another blast cut the pilot off. It was followed by a fast-paced beeping that was swiftly drowned out by the sounds of chaos: wild shrieks and the twisting of metal.

Finally, only static remained. The familiar hissing that had put Ben to sleep all those nights. Only this time, he heard something low in the background. It was faint, barely discernable.

Was it sobbing? Or giggling? It could only have come from a child.

Ben switched off the radio before he could know for sure.

ABBY'S LITTLE TEA PARTY

"**C**an I go, mom? Can I please?"

Ginny was waiting patiently on the porch, her layers of golden hair sparkling in the sunlight.

"A tea party?" my mother asked, a thin smirk across her face.

I rolled my eyes. Was it so hard for her to just say yes?

It was my first tea party invite, and to be honest, I never felt like I was ever missing out. I wasn't that kind of girl. Playing make-believe and dress-up—it all felt awkward and forced. Despite my indifference, tonight, I was inclined to give it a shot. I figured I'd try something new for a change before time had passed me by and I was too old to partake in the activity.

And really, it was all for Ginny.

Mom grabbed my hand, pulling me a few steps inside the house. "I don't know, Abby. This is pretty last minute. Can you two plan a day next week instead?

My body collapsed to the floor. "Mom, please! It's only for a couple of hours."

She stood expressionless in the doorway. I tugged on her cardigan, pleading my case. I pointed to the other kids pedaling their bikes across our street. It was still early. It wasn't fair.

Mom bit her lower lip, the cogs spinning in her head. I just wondered in what direction. She sighed. "Dinner's already in the oven, honey. And your father isn't even home yet from work."

"Please..." I begged, groveling at my mother's feet. Eyelashes flickering, puppy dog stare.

She turned towards Ginny, "Where are your parents, young lady?"

Ginny smiled. "We live down the block, Mrs. Huntington. Mom's cooking a casserole for tonight, but it won't be done for a while. And Dad—well, he's doing something boring in the garage, tinkering with the car or something."

We both rolled our eyes and spoke together, "Dad things."

I pulled my mother closer, whispering in her ear. "Please," I urged. "Just save me dinner, just for tonight."

She looked past Ginny, tapping the metal door frame with her freshly coated fingernails. "Okay, fine. But you two better be careful."

"Yes!" I erupted.

She hollered at us, "Make sure you look both ways before you cross the road!". We were already off the porch, skipping down the driveway together. "And be home by dark!"

Ginny and I giggled as we exited the cul-de-sac, passing the rows of cookie-cutter homes. The neighborhood was alive with children: groups of them marking up their driveways with colorful sticks of chalk, others leaping through tall arcs of water spraying out of sprinklers. They shrieked as the cold stream hit their bodies. Summer was in full bloom.

"Which one is yours?" I asked Ginny.

"It's the brown one. Just down the road." She pointed to one of the beige duplexes on the left side of the street. "But that's not where we're going, though, silly."

"Where are we going?"

There was a man sitting on a lawn chair halfway up his drive-way. His gut hung out of his shirt. We stopped to read the logo: *The*

Dad, The Myth, The Legend. He raised his open can of beer to us and smiled. We hurried away, giggling.

"Down by the ravine. You ever been?"

"No." I stopped in the middle of the street. "I mean... yes. Just never without my parents.

"Oh, we'll be fine, Abby. Don't worry. My friends are already down there. And we'll be back before anybody notices."

I frowned for a moment, but Ginny pulled me along the road. She flashed her gleaming set of perfect white teeth, and the trepidation had been tamed.

This neighborhood was all I'd ever known. I knew all the playgrounds, every store, like the back of my hand. But still, there were corners left unexplored, pockets of uncharted territory hidden within the manicured avenues and streets.

I was amazed by the confidence of the young girl. Three weeks in town and she strutted through the neighborhood like she was the mayor. Three weeks and she already had friends. I should have been the one showing her around, introducing her to my circle of people. Only that circle didn't exist.

Instead, Ginny held my hand, twirling me around a lamppost. "Let's go, silly. We're already late!" I followed her magnetic presence.

We chased each other across the road, towards the outer edge of our neighborhood. We skipped past a couple more blocks of houses, eventually taking a right down a paved pathway. We narrowly collided with a cyclist who grunted back in anger. We continued down the path towards a park bench atop a hill. The trees tapered down a lengthy slope. Fallen leaves and rotting logs littered the steep decline.

"It's just by the water," she assured me. Glancing back, she offered me her hand. "We'll go slow, I promise." Our fingers interlocked, and we proceeded down the hill.

Ginny led us through the forested obstacle course. We dodged outstretched branches with razor sharp tips that nicked tiny holes through our cotton t-shirts, overturned logs, and endless piles of leaves. Skittish squirrels retreated up the trunks of their trees. Each crunching, crinkling step was more cautious than the next.

Once we made it to the water, the terrain flattened. Hard, solid ground became boggy marsh. I wiggled my toes and heard a squish, each appendage swimming through a puddle in my sneakers. "Mom is going to kill me," I groaned.

Ginny glanced down at her browned shoes. She pouted playfully. "They'll dry off before we get back. Maybe we can wash them down at my house afterward."

We were sheltered from the sun by the overhanging branches, the light fragmented and chopped in slits and slants amongst the shadows.

She pointed to a small clearing in the forest. A willow tree stood alone by the water, its vast root system jutting in and out of the mud. Off in the distance, under the tree, was a circular table with an elegant white tablecloth draped over top.

"We're here! Finally!" she declared.

A lady in a glimmering red dress was setting the table. She waved, her hair tight in curly, burgundy locks. Another little girl had her back to us. She was crouched over and playing with something at the edge of the water.

Ginny introduced me to the woman, "Leela, this is Abby."

We hugged. "So glad you could join us, dear," she said. "I've heard so much about you."

"Nice to meet you, Miss," I replied, glancing over at Ginny. I was surprised by her age; she looked to be older than my mom.

"And you know Teddy?" Leela said, pointing to a large stuffed teddy bear occupying one of the empty stools. Teddy looked like he had been well loved: stuffing poked out of the seams of one of his arms, and his button nose hung loosely from a tiny, dangling thread.

Seeing the doll turned Abby's spine into a thin trail of ice; she had lost the bear years ago. It was her favorite toy when she was a child, but it had long been forgotten. She vaguely remembered the fateful afternoon she had dragged him to the park, and he had just... disappeared. Now all the memories of him were swirling up.

"Is this everyone?" I whispered to Ginny.

She nodded.

"Oh," I replied, an uneasy feeling settling in the pit of my stomach. *This was all? No one from school?*

"Let us start, then," Leela announced. She placed a tiara on top of Ginny's head, the silver gems dazzling in the sunlight. Ginny hopped up and down with glee. "Grab one for Abby, too!"

I declined, shaking my head. Far too girly for me.

We took our seats: the three of us and Teddy. The sun's rays danced off the water, the soothing sound of the stream filling the silence. There was the occasional splash from the girl off in the distance. She seemed content playing by herself.

"How was everyone's day?" Leela asked, grabbing the handle of a white porcelain teapot. It had a deep blue ivy pattern wrapped along the base that reminded me of my grandmother's set.

"Teddy says good," Ginny giggled. And I caught myself staring into her misty blue eyes. A tiny web of wrinkles emerged from the corners of them as she smiled. I grinned back.

One by one, Leela tipped the spout and pretended to pour. She handed the cups to Ginny who passed them around to the guests.

"Besides school, I guess it was okay," I half-heartedly chimed in.

"Well, that's good. School can be quite a drag at this age," Leela said. "I promise you, it gets better." Once everyone had their cup, she raised hers in the air. "Cheers, everyone." The porcelain clinked together.

I brought the rim to my mouth and tipped the cup.

It should have been empty, but it wasn't.

My face went pale as something foul ran down my throat. Something viscous that burned with a sharp chemical odor. I coughed, trying to rid my mouth of the taste, trying to spit whatever it was out. The cup fell, rolling across the table on its side. It left no trail of liquid as it rolled past Teddy.

Ginny rushed over. "What's wrong? Are you okay?"

I reached for the cup, placing it upright. I rubbed my index finger inside the curved bowl.

Bone dry.

My stomach simmered like a pot of boiling water. I clutched a handful of tablecloth as the ground began to teeter.

"Not a big fan of tea?" Leela chuckled.

Ginny's freckled face was now blurred and distorted. I toppled backward off the stool into the soft grass.

My mind slipped away, just the sounds of the wild taking over—the steady dribbling of the stream. Magpies chirping. The splashing of water.

"Now we can begin," Leela declared.

❖

I awoke to a soft sweeping feeling, a tickling against my neck. Long, feathery lances drooped down from the canopy. I batted them away from my face as they brushed against my cheek. The appendages swayed from side to side like the eerie arm of a metronome, gently swaying along with the breeze. Sitting upright on my stool, my vision spun. Ginny and Leela were deep in conversation. I couldn't make out their muffled whispers.

"Abby? Are you okay?" Ginny called out.

I coughed. My throat still burned with the rawness of exposed flesh to flame.

She turned to Leela, "Thank God. I think she's back."

Leela winked in my direction. "You're missing the party, Abby. You sure everything is alright?"

My lips quivered. "I want to go home."

"You're not having fun?" Ginny frowned. "I don't want you to go home just yet. Let's wait a little while. I'm sure you'll feel better!"

Tears trickled down my cheek. "I feel sick."

The stool wobbled when I tried to steady my feet. Before I could turn, something gripped me. The sweeping limbs had wrapped themselves around me, their squeeze tight and unforgiving. I lost feeling in my arms.

Raspy shrieks escaped from my throat. Birds took flight from nearby trees, but there was little else in response.

"We're almost done, Abby," Leela promised. "Don't worry. Then you can go home."

Ginny's lips were now pursed.

"Sit down beside your friend, Ginny," Leela insisted.

She cautiously took a seat.

Leela continued, a smile flashing through the mesh of her fascinator headpiece, "Oh, Abby. Poor Abby. You're not like the other girls, are you?"

"What do you mean?" I asked, my voice shallow and shaky.

"Tell me, what do you think of Ginny?"

"Uh... I don't know what you mean? I think she's cool. And fun."

"I think Abby's cool too," Ginny chimed in. "So please, can we go home now?"

Leela poured herself another cup of air, her pinky extended. "Ginny, your friend looks very scared. Don't you think you should go over there and give her a hug?"

Without hesitation, she walked over and wrapped her arms around me.

"Good," Leela said.

A brisk breeze blew in through the trees. The light trickling in through the treetops was now slivers, quickly fading into darkness.

"Now give her a kiss," Leela ordered. Ginny squinted, her face sour. "Why?"

"Go on now. Just a little peck."

She glared back at Leela. "And what if I don't?"

"I asked nicely, Ginny!" Leela shrieked, nearly sending Ginny off her stool. Another brisk breath of air whisked in from the trees behind us. The trail of their footsteps was now shrouded in darkness.

Ginny stood up slowly and reluctantly obliged. Her lips felt smooth as they quivered against my skin.

"Not on the cheek. On the lips."

Ginny looked frightened by the sharpness in her tone. She objected.

"Do what I say!" Leela barked, her hands slamming against the table in a sudden jerk. The cups tottered on their plates. "I won't be asking again."

Ginny's eyes were wide and innocent. A tear trickled down her cheek. She hesitated, her body shaking.

Leela took another sip from her cup, her legs crossed. "We're still waiting."

She eventually gave in to the request and puckered up her lips. She leaned in, slowly. My heart jittered as our lips met. There was a sudden splash of warmth, a tingly feeling. A quick second of bliss. And when it was over, Leela was standing over us, applauding.

Ginny wiped her mouth.

"There you go, girls. See—it wasn't that bad? Now was it?"

Before I could answer, long fingers crawled up from behind Ginny's shoulders. They snatched her hair and yanked her to the floor. The little girl from the water dragged Ginny towards the edge of the ravine. Her long, soaked hair trailed down to the back of her knees.

"Stop!" I shrieked. The leafy branchlets confined my movement, rooting me to my seat.

Leela cackled. "Go on, then. Save your little friend."

At once, the tension was released. The arms of the tree withdrew, recoiling into the thick nest of the canopy.

I ran.

Ginny's head was being lowered into the water.

"Get your hands off of her!" I screamed.

The little girl ignored my desperate plea. She plunged Ginny's head into the stream, creating violent ripples and splashes that spread across the body of water. Her body was thrashed about easily like a ragdoll.

The strength of the girl was immense. She had her prey in her grasp, an alligator deep in the swamp. I couldn't see the girl's face behind her long, dripping bangs, but I could see her two fistfuls of golden hair that were forcing Ginny under.

I connected with a sold punch to the back of her head. She growled as I climbed her back, trying to throw off her center of gravity. She didn't so much as stumble or break her gaze.

During the melee, I noticed the dress. It was a hideous mess of pink and purple frills, a spitting image of the one my mom had tried to make me wear to my brother's Christening.

After another hard blow, she finally turned in my direction. I stumbled backward when I saw her face. Or lack of face.

It was an empty void of skin, heinous folds of wrinkled flesh.

Leela caught up to us, squeezing my arm from behind. "Well, you're going to have to do better than that!"

She tugged on my arm as we approached the faceless girl. With all my strength, I grabbed onto her hair, chunks of greasy, soaked locks intertwined between my fingers. Leela did the same. The girl finally let go of Ginny. She fought and kicked and screamed as we forced her head into the frigid water. She flailed violently as her poofy dress whipped across the surface.

Loud, choking gasps. Gurgling cries.

I felt her skull thud against the jagged rocks beneath. Never once did I have the urge to stop.

Leela spoke in a soothing tone, "That's a good girl. Let her go."

After a long struggle, her body went limp. We watched her float away downstream. My hands fell to my knees, my lungs heaving in and out. Before I had a chance to recover, I was knocked into the water too. The electric chill surged through my body. My lungs burned, the water sloshing around in my chest.

That's a good girl.

Let her go.

I woke up. Shivering. Just a kid under a willow tree. The magpie's chorus was replaced by crickets. The sun was no more, swallowed up by the darkness and the sprinkling of a million stars.

There was a faint light atop the hill. I stepped into the twilight—drenched, exhausted, and alone. I started my ascent, blindly stumbling through the forest. When I made it to the park bench underneath the lamppost, I noticed that I had Teddy clutched to my chest.

It was a long walk home, the streets vacant and dead. Once I made it to the residential area, I followed the rows of lampposts, the route home burned into my memory.

Mom was so upset she barely spoke to me. The cop cars were all sent home.

But the worst part about it all wasn't the grounding. I knew I wouldn't see the light of day for a long time. The worst part about it all was Ginny. Everything had changed.

She barely recognized me anymore. She didn't look at me, didn't speak to me. She denies everything about that night. We are complete strangers now.

Maybe it's a defense mechanism of hers in order to deal with the trauma. I don't know. But my God has it been frustrating.

Because it happened. Whatever it was, whoever her friends were. And I can't just simply forget because there are still so many questions.

All I know is that in my dreams, I see us. Abby and Ginny. Dancing under the willow, a light breeze whistling through the trees.

And the faceless girl floats away, peacefully, downstream.

THE MAN AT THE DINER

The bell jingled above the entryway as the door to the diner swung open. Like clockwork, the man strode in.

9:00 AM. Rain or shine.

He approached one of the booths by the window, hung his coat on the nearby rack, and slid his bowler hat across the table. I watched as he calmly pulled open a newspaper.

After a few minutes, I walked over, his lips silently mouthing the words he was reading on the page.

I hardly needed to ask the question, but I decided to indulge us both:

"What can I get for you, sir?"

It was the same order, every time:

Two scrambled eggs, beans, and hash with a side order of back bacon.

A cup of coffee: two creams, one sugar.

The man had shown up for months, always quietly finding a seat at one of the booths. He was always alone, his only interactions seemingly to order his refills of coffee. There wasn't much more of a routine to speak of: after flipping through the morning paper, he would just sit and gaze out the window. This in itself was not unusual—we sure had our share of regulars at our little roadside diner—but none quite like this man. It was hard to explain.

"Still in town for work, I see."

He glanced up from the sports section, the wrinkles on his thick and leathery face like etches of time worn through an elephant's hide. "No rest for the wicked."

I poured him another round of java, wisps of steam billowing from his mug. I softly placed my hand over his for a moment, his knuckles bony and ice-cold.

"Today's the day. I can feel it."

He offered a gentle smile. "Thanks, Lydia. Me too."

My shift flew by, the day largely uneventful. The typical rush of people at Dawn's Diner came and went: the senior crowd, the truck drivers, and the family vacationers. The restaurant always seemed to attract a steady flow of customers.

The checkered floors were a little more scuffed, the bubble-gum walls were a little more faded, and the red leather booths had a few more cracks, but overall, the place had largely stood the test of time. We had survived just off the highway since the grand opening in the late '70s.

I frequented the place often as a child. Grandma used to take me for root beer floats on the weekends. These fond memories are the reason why I chose to work here all these years. With a bad back now and carpal tunnel (and all of the excuses in the world to retire), something kept me coming back to Dawn's Diner. If it wasn't for my job, I would be on the other side of the counter, putzing around with a coffee and a side of eggs. At least this way I was staying busy and making some pocket change.

Today was shaping up to be just like the others. Not much changes in a place like this.

While I finished wiping down another table, I glanced over at the man in the booth. He had a dull expression on his face, his body unmoved. He was staring out the window like a lost puppy.

As the sun set, the streetlights in the parking lot began to turn on. Before it got too dark, the man would settle his tab and pack up his things. Then I would see him bright and early in the morning, caught in the same small-town time loop that I was in.

I brought back a tray of dirty dishes to the kitchen. When I rounded the corner, the man was standing.

"Can I get you anything, honey? Need me to break a bill?"

The bell jingled.

"He's here," the man stated, his eyes wide. He was transfixed by the sight of the young man who had just entered. He was a tall, sinewy fellow with a thick mop of tangled hair. We watched him walk to a nearby table by the registers, plop his backpack on the counter, and head straight for the washroom.

"Are you sure it's him?" I asked.

He nodded.

"That is excellent. Just excellent!"

The old man had very few words, but from the little information he had shared with me and the months of waiting that had occurred, I felt a sudden rush of emotion that overwhelmed my system. Wiping tears from my eyes, I said, "Say hi to him for me, okay?"

The man's face remained unchanged. He looked stunned, his body stiff, his feet planted to the floor. A tingle of embarrassment seeped into my rosy cheeks.

"It will be fine," I assured him. "Just talk to him."

In an instant, his expression had soured. He leaned in close to whisper:

"*You need to leave.*"

"Excuse me?"

"*Now!*" he hissed. "Let me be with my son."

The wiry man exited the washroom. We watched him pull up a chair at the table, nervously fidgeting with his hands.

The old man's eyes darted from me to the hallway, then back to me again, insisting that I leave. He took a deep breath and then exhaled slowly.

Startled by the man's scathing tone, I chose to honor his wishes. What did I really care, anyway? The reunion would go on without me. I stepped away, heading towards the hallway to the kitchen. I was nearly at my manager's office when the lights began to flicker.

Then came the blast. The devastating sound of shattered glass and shrill screams filled the air. The diner suddenly went black.

There was instant chaos in the hallways, people frantically pushing and clawing their way to the back exit. The alarm blared in high-pitched dings as water rained down from the sprinklers. The lights flickered on again, only for a moment, before fizzling back out. More panicked shrieks followed as everyone struggled to escape.

After what felt like an eternity, I made it outside with the stars and the steady breeze. A little sweaty, but otherwise unharmed, I wove through the small groups of people huddled together, many of whom were soaked and just trying to catch their breath. I passed by some of my coworkers who looked shell-shocked, some of them crying, others shakily holding their cellphones to their ears. I trudged towards the front of the building.

A pillar of flames crackled inside the dark confines of the restaurant. The flames were fanning out, unperturbed by the spitting of water from the sprinklers. There was a glint of movement in the embers, shadows of something cutting in and out of the light before a chunk of the roof caved in. The emphatic crash sent sparks into the air.

I couldn't look away.

The parking lot began to fill as curious bystanders spotted the commotion from the freeway, and patrons of the restaurant slowly made their way to the front of the building.

"Lydia! Oh my goodness. I'm so glad that you're okay." Ruth, the restaurant manager, closed the distance and held me in a bear hug.

"I'm good, love. Just rattled. How about you? Did everyone make it out okay?"

"I think so. It was a crude headcount, but I think I got everyone. What the hell happened?"

"I ain't got no damn clue," she said, glancing down at her cell phone. "Thought it came from the kitchen at first—Gerry forgetting to turn off the gas or something stupid. Wouldn't put it past that dimwit. I was pretty certain, but that's not what some of the others are saying..."

I paused. "What do you mean?"

The fire trucks sirens roared from the highway as the red vehicles rolled into the parking lot.

"I overheard someone saying they saw a man."

Four firefighters hopped out from one of the trucks lugging a massive hose atop their shoulders. Another group stormed the entrance.

"A man?" I asked, my voice trembling.

"Yup. A man," she confirmed. "Blown up and everything. Completely engulfed in flames. Right out in the open." She shook her head. "Sounds like a whole lot of nonsense to me."

Water flooded out of the nozzle in a fierce stream. Two of the firefighters instructed us to step back, pushing the line of spectators away from the building.

I bit my tongue. I contemplated heading home to get some rest, but as the flames began to simmer down, I decided to confide in Ruth.

"Ruth," I said. "You know the man who comes in every morning? The old man with the hat. You know the one I'm talking about? The one who stays by the window all day." She raised one of her eyebrows as I continued, "I think... I... I don't know. But I think he might have something to do with this."

The police sirens were deafening as the squad cars ripped into the parking lot.

"I ain't seen no one like that, Lydia."

My heart raced. "Ruth. Come on. He sits at the booths all day. Every day."

We argued about the man for a long time, the smoke heavy and clinging to our clothing. Most of the crowd had headed home.

"I know bout' all the regulars, darling. Don't go quizzing me. Ain't no man shows up every day and I don't recognize him."

Now my blood was beginning to boil. "Ruth. Seriously. This isn't funny."

Equipped with a fire-retardant suit and gas mask, one of the crime scene investigators was lugging a charred backpack out of the building in a clear plastic bag labeled: "EVIDENCE". What remained of the backpack were chunks of burnt fabric. It was clearly unzipped, revealing the barrel of an assault rifle covered in ash. The weapon was pressed up against the sealed plastic.

Ruth placed her hand on my shoulder, "Get some rest, my dear."

We didn't hear much about the fire for a couple of months. The coroners and fire inspectors were left baffled, attributing the event to something they termed SHC or "Spontaneous Human Combustion". It was an incredibly rare occurrence that left a lot of unanswered questions. Witnesses claimed they saw the young man go up in flames. It was sudden immolation without a plausible source of ignition. There were trace levels of gunpowder found on the man's rifle and on the lining of the man's bag, but the fire experts still couldn't trace the source of the spark. No bullets had been fired.

The mystery still looms over our town today with many tourists making it a point to visit the diner.

Operations were shut down indefinitely for the better part of a year while construction crews worked through the rubble. It took a while, but Dawn's Diner finally got its much-needed makeover.

The old booths were replaced, new jukeboxes were put in, and the kitchen was completely remodeled. The owners opted to keep the iconic '70s style with some much-needed additional upgrades. We were a tourist attraction now, after all.

It's still the old Dawn's Diner with a modern twist. The friendly family establishment aura still remains, but the mystery of that night makes the place feel... different.

That's how I would describe myself now: the same old Lydia, but different.

Business is as booming as ever, with new faces mixed in with the old. I am grateful I survived the fire. I truly am.

But I often catch myself staring out the diner window, looking for someone I hardly knew.

I never saw the man again.

BUYER'S REMORSE

"Okay—three-two-one, GO!"

We stabbed a hole through our cans with our pocket knives, placing our mouths to the crude openings as the beer spurted out. Jordy's reflexes were a half second too slow, and his shirt suffered the consequences. Typical rookie mistake. I downed the drink a good five seconds before Jordy finished. Colt came in last, a few seconds behind him.

"It's not fair. You guys started earlier," Colt complained. The loser always complained.

I tossed him the bottle of Fireball. "Quit making excusessss and take your shot."

Colt took a swig and winced. Jordy laughed, playfully massaging his shoulder.

We were sitting in the back of Jordy's '91 Ford F-150. It was more rust than truck these days, but the old girl always seemed to get the job done. There was silence as we stared at the open sky. Over the years, we shared some amazing summers together, and tonight was no exception. But there was an air of sadness in the warm breeze. Come fall time, we would all be going our separate ways: Jordy heading out east, Colt destined for the Midwest, and me, stuck in this lousy town. Alone.

The boys were heading off to college, and part of me knew that these summer nights would never be the same again.

I popped open another can and took a long sip.

"Boys... Boys! We best be going before it's too friggin' late!" Jordy hopped off the truck, staggering toward the festivities. The sun was setting a beautiful blood-red orange.

Colt held his hand out. "Okay. Okay. Just let me make a quick call first."

"Jesus, Colt," I scoffed. "It's *one night*, dude. You can do without her for one night."

"It will be quick," he promised.

Jordy rolled his eyes at me in response, and I chuckled. Long-term relationships were for suckers as far as we were concerned, but Colt seemed to really love this chick. By our standards, they were practically married.

We staggered through the gravel lot with beers in hand, leaving Colt to hover around the truck with his phone to his ear. We weaved through the rows of vehicles packed together.

Every summer, the town of Hinton hosts a pop-up shop for vendors at the local farmers' market. It's a week-long event that excites the soccer mom in every family across the county. The farmer's field was packed with people: two lanes of merchants stretched all the way to the fence line. We stumbled through the crowds, eyeing the typical crap on display: every type of fruit and vegetable, homemade arts and crafts, and the occasional honey vendor.

We heard a familiar voice in the crowd.

"Woah." Colt had caught up to us and was holding what looked like the skull of a chimpanzee in his palm. He raised it in the air like he was offering it to the gods. Jordy and I darted through the maze of people to get to him.

A man startled us from behind the booth. "You break it, you buy it, chaps."

He was dressed in a brown tweed blazer and a black homburg hat: a middle-aged man with a nineteenth-century style. It was rare to see this type of hipster in this neck of the woods.

"Colt, you idiot!" Jordy laughed.

He apologized, placing the skull down gently.

"No worries at all. You boys look like you've had some fun tonight," the man grinned. "Take a look around. You won't find items like this anywhere in the world." He began to polish a mason jar filled with a grainy, turquoise liquid. "The name's Mr. Griff if you have any questions."

He was right. His collection was eclectic, to say the least. An array of items was laid across the table in an orderly fashion: labeled containers filled with various powders and oils, ancient, handcrafted instruments, skulls of several exotic animals, carved statues, masks and dolls from different countries, jars of floating things that I couldn't identify. I looked over at my bewildered friends, their mouths wide open.

"How did you get these items?" Jordy asked. He proceeded to knock one of the jars off the table with his elbow. Mr. Griff's quick reflexes saved it from hitting the gravel. He shook his head in disgust, "What the hell did I tell you? You hard of hearing?" He gave the jar a gentle polish and placed it back on the table. For a moment, I thought he was going to tell us to scram, but he kept his cool, and instead, he leaned in closer. "I am a traveler of sorts, a collector really. I have a fascination for strange antiques and a passion for bartering. I was planning on passing through this town actually until I spotted the flyer for this event at one of the local diners off the freeway." He brushed his auburn hair behind his ears and shifted towards me. "That one's a real beauty, isn't it?"

I was eyeing a peculiar box in the front row. I admired the careful, delicate intricacies of the design. It was an immaculate gold, and it carried a strong smell of tobacco and incense that I had never encountered before.

"This cigar case was crafted in the Arabian Peninsula." He gloated, "It's over six hundred years old, you know. Truly one of a kind."

Colt joked, "It sure would make a great addition to your bong shelf, Caden."

I snickered, punching him in the arm. "How much for it?"

Mr. Griff paused, running his fingers through his mustache. "Really hard to put a price on something like this." He took a minute, pacing back and forth behind the booth. "I would be willing to part ways with it for five hundred."

I gulped. My hand fished through the inside of my pocket: a stick of gum, two crumpled up twenties, and some lint. *Really wish we bought less booze*, I thought. In desperation, I pulled the boys aside, forming a huddle.

"There's no way he's serious?" Colt whispered.

Jordy agreed, "That's bloody robbery!"

"*Shhh*. How much do you guys have on you? I swear, I'll pay you back." Jordy placed a twenty in my hand. I hated taking money from him, but I was desperate. Mostly because I knew his mother would sniff around. They never had much of anything growing up—his dad split before he was barely able to walk—so she was always pinching pennies and watching their finances like a hawk. I made a mental note of the amount and prayed I would remember in my inebriated state.

Colt rummaged up two tens and a five dollar bill out of his weathered leather wallet.

"Maybe we can pass that gum off as 'vintage'," Colt joked. It was a grand total of eighty-five dollars.

I spun out of the huddle and approached the table. Mr. Griff was in a conversation with another customer. My drunk ass blurted out, "Eighty-five dollars, sir, and not a penny more!" slamming the wrinkled bills on top of the table for dramatic effect. Colt and Jordy snickered. The merchandise wobbled, but luckily nothing toppled over.

Mr. Griff wasn't laughing, though. He seemed to absorb the lowball offer, standing in a peculiar silence. He grabbed the bills, one by one, but instead of passing over the item on the table, he reached into his suitcase and handed me something else.

"All sales final." He smiled, leaning towards us. "Now get the fuck out of here. *Now!*" He lunged at us, but he missed. The abrupt scream sent us in a direct sprint toward the vehicle. People stopped and stared as we cut through the crowd of traffic.

The world was spinning. My heart pounded in my chest as we finally made our way to the truck. Only then did we laugh—an uncontrollable, deranged chuckle. It was a rare kind of relief, a feeling only experienced when surviving a narrow escape.

Three drunk heaping messes rolling around in the dirt. We laughed and laughed, clutching our insides until our lungs ached.

Our friend Mary spotted us in the parking lot and kindly offered to drop us off at my apartment for the evening. On the ride home, I examined the item I had purchased. It was a lower-quality product than the box that was advertised, but it was a cigar case, nonetheless. The main difference was in the material. This model was not gold, but a brass veneer. It was also filthy, with the outer layer beginning to corrode along the edges, but the intricate pattern was very similar. There were constellations and planets etched into the outside cover of the box along with some strange foreign lettering.

Jordy and myself helped carry Colt up the stairs of the apartment. After he hit the sofa, Jordy darted for the washroom and made it his home for the evening.

I took a hit and laid in my bed. As the THC entered my bloodstream, I rotated the box from side to side. Something rattled within its confines. I took a t-shirt from the floor and wiped the black dust off the surface. That's when I noticed it was locked. I laughed to myself—I guess the key must have cost extra. Searching my room, I found a sim card ejector pin and began tinkering with the lock. It finally clicked open after an hour of jiggling the mechanism. Inside was a pipe made of wood and a long piece of parchment paper. It was rolled up, containing writing in Arabic script. I put the paper to the side and rinsed the pipe. I wasted no time grabbing the weed from the dresser and stuffing it inside the bowl. The high was unlike anything I had ever experienced. My head started to thump. I imagined all of the people that had used the pipe over the years. Five generations of degenerates.

The light coming from the ceiling seemed to refract and bend at strange angles. But that wasn't the strangest occurrence. I sat up, noticing the smoke coming out of the pipe. It was the darkest cloud of black: a thick, inky obsidian. It spiraled towards the ceiling, collecting and molding itself into a figure. Then it appeared.

"Ahhhh, at last! Thank you, good sir. You did the right thing; I can assure you."

I crept back as far as I could to the back wall. "What the hell are you? Get the fuck away!"

"Sorry, how rude of me! My name is Oriah. You have graciously summoned me, sir, freeing me from my confines. For that, I am eternally grateful. There is nothing to be afraid of. If anything, you should be excited. You now wield incredible power."

I pinched myself as hard as I could.

The jinn's features resembled the head of a goat and the body of a gorilla. Shrouded in smoke, its horns nearly touched the ceiling.

It floated closer.

"Well, I summon you back to wherever you came from. That is my wish."

Oriah erupted in laughter.

"That is a good one, sir. But that's not how this works. Allow me to explain: you have summoned me, and in return, a series of events have unfolded. You have a big decision to make that I have the power to fulfill."

"So, you're a genie then? I thought I could wish for anything?"

"No, unfortunately, that is not how this works, either. This contract has a narrower scope. Pending my release, you are granted the authority of selecting a replacement for my imprisonment."

"Imprisonment?"

"Precisely! Choose wisely. I've spent many a century stuck in this dastardly contraption." He floated over to the box and inspected it. "This individual will take my place within the confines of the pipe and the box. These items are magically bound together. They will remain immortal until their summoning."

"And if I select no one?"

He snickered. "With all due respect, sir, that would be a grave mistake. *You* would become the replacement."

I scoffed at the entity, "This is bullshit. You're lying."

"I assure you, I am not. If you want proof, go and look for your friends." I froze in terror. "Colt? Jordy?"

I rushed out of the bedroom—there was no one on the sofa. I whipped open the door to the washroom, and it was empty. They had vanished into thin air.

I grabbed my phone and started dialing. Both calls went straight to voicemail.

"Bring them back. This isn't funny."

"Not to worry, friend. Honestly. They are being held in trust, pending my release."

"What the fuck does that even mean?"

He followed me into the living room, floating above the sofa. Colt and Jordy's backpacks were half open on the floor, just as they had left them.

"Did you not read the agreement?" Oriah retrieved the piece of parchment paper that was lying on my bed. "I didn't have much reading material options," Oriah laughed. "So, I can recite it to you, if I must. They are being held in the 'in-between', the transit area for the living and the dead."

I imagined the terror on their faces if all of this was true.

Oriah continued, "Again, don't worry. They are completely safe. I require them as collateral, in case you don't follow through. Call it extra incentive to find my replacement. I am well within my rights, as they were parties to the sale but not the deemed summoner. It is all in there," Oriah smugly mentioned, handing me the crumpled-up paper.

Anger simmered deep inside of me. "Well, I choose Mr. Griff. The bastard who sold me this forsaken box."

Oriah applauded. "That is an excellent choice! An excellent choice, indeed." There was a long pause. "However... Mr. Griff is not eligible, unfortunately. And there would be no sweeter feeling than for me to send that man to his doom."

"What do you mean *not eligible*? That is my selection."

He sighed. "Unfortunately, your selection must be human. Mr. Griff does not fit that... criteria."

I brushed my hand nervously through my hair.

The mysterious being continued, "He is what you humans may call 'otherworldly'. An inter-dimensional swindler, of sorts. An evil twat, to say the least. He is the one who scammed me into confinement for all of these years."

"This all makes no sense."

The jinn shrugged. "With all due respect, sir, I think you need to look at this from a different angle. Have you ever wanted to hurt someone so deeply for the wrongs they had committed against you? Most people only dream about sweet revenge. This is so much bigger than wishing death upon someone. You have a real opportunity here, at *vengeance*. Do not squander this opportunity."

The darkness of those words wove itself deeply into my soul. I've hated a ton of people throughout my life. I may have wished misfortune upon those individuals. Hell, if I was being honest, even death. But there is a difference between fantasizing and acting upon dark impulses. To be imprisoned potentially for eternity—I couldn't imagine what one would have to do to deserve such a fate.

I sat in shock, struck by a stroke of guilt for Colt and Jordy's wellbeing. They had nothing to do with this mess. It was supposed to be a fun night, goofing off with pals. Now I faced the heaviest decision of my life, with theirs weighing in the balance.

"As per the agreement, you have twenty-four hours." He grinned, "Pleasure doing business with you."

As the jinn vaporized into the night, I walked to the fridge and grabbed another beer.

EXOTIC ENCOUNTERS

Seeing Nicole that night was like spotting a snow leopard in the wild. I nearly pinched myself in disbelief. It had been over forty years since I last saw her face; yet there she was, sitting at the end of the bar like she had never left.

She looked as stunning as ever: wrapped in a thick mink coat that hung to the floor, her tan leather boots dangling from the stool. Her hair was shorter now—it was curly and a shimmering silver instead of the long locks of blonde that I remembered—but I knew it was undoubtedly her.

I stared down at my drink, contemplating whether I should approach her or not. We were old people now in the twilight of our lives. I wondered what I could even say. So much time had passed.

Curiosity got the better of me, and I took a brave gulp. I meandered over to her, beer in hand.

"*Nicole*? Is that you?"

She didn't look up from her phone.

My face ran hot with embarrassment. The fight-or-flight response in me screamed run.

"Nicole?" I repeated, gently tapping her shoulder.

She looked up, and we locked eyes: those lush emerald beads that still captured a place in my heart after all these years.

"*Eddie?* Oh my God, Eddie!" She hugged me and my anxiety melted away. "How long has it been?"

"I still had hair the last time we met. So, safe to say, it's been a little while."

Nicole nearly spat out her drink. "You haven't changed one bit. And this bar—it's almost exactly how I remembered it!"

She wasn't lying; Mckailey's was a spitting image of its old self. It was a relic that had been kept in the Mckailey family, passed down from generation to generation dating back to my grandfather's time. It wasn't the hippest establishment anymore, but it was one I held dear to my heart. I showed up every Sunday for a quick pint. It had become a sort of tradition, allowing me to reflect on my week and momentarily escape the hecticness of my family. I think deep down, I secretly came back hoping I would spot her here again.

"Do you remember when we stole Lyle's father's pickup truck and drove it here? We were begging Katherine for a drink."

I chuckled. "How could I forget the desperation? It's owned by her son, David, now. That sort of thing would never slide anymore."

We both laughed as a Luther Vandross song played on the jukebox. His silky-smooth voice brought us closer, the saxophones carrying us away. Besides a couple of stragglers, the bar was dead.

"You remember this spot in particular?" I pointed above to a small bell hanging from the support beam. It looked like it belonged in an old church; it was rusted with a long crack along the side and a rope dangled down from the ceiling. It was Katherine's darling, but the damn thing stuck out like a sore thumb. It was my darling too. I used to scope the spot out back in the day, back when I still had 'game'.

Nicole's face turned bright pink. "Oh, I'm old... but not *that* old."

The antique hanging from the rafters had served me well over the years.

Memories of the "first-kiss bell" made me feel achingly warm.

I ordered another round as we continued our conversation. Nicole was only passing through to spend some time at her daughter's place in the city. She filled me in on her life: she had two daughters from two different marriages and three grandkids, with one more on the way. She pulled out pictures from her purse, and we admired their cuteness together. She had traveled the world extensively and worked abroad for a number of years.

"Sounds like you really did it," I smiled. "You lived the big, colorful life that you always talked about."

Her cheeks flared a rosy red again. There was a pause as we both took a sip of our drinks. "Geez, I've been talking your ear off, Eddie. How about yourself? What have you been up to all these years?"

"Me? Oh, not much, really," I said in between sips. "I never left. I own all of the Rutterson pharmacies in town now. Got myself a wife, Karen, and a white picket fence. We have a daughter, Mckenzie, and she has two granddaughters that we spoil to death." It was my turn for show-and-tell as I pulled out my wallet. "Their names are Chloe and Veronica."

She smiled as she examined the pictures closely.

"We are actually celebrating Mckenzie's birthday with the little ones this evening."

"Oh my goodness, they are *so* adorable. How old are they if you don't mind me asking? And what race? They look so beautiful."

"Chloe is four, and Veronica will be two in a couple of weeks. Mckenzie married a Filipino fellow, so they are my little halfies," I joked.

"Well, they look extremely exotic. So precious."

An awkward moment dragged on as I mustered the courage to ask the question that had been eating away at me all these years.

"So... Nicole. I gotta ask... why did you leave without saying goodbye?"

She stared at her empty glass, rolling the ice cubes around. The jukebox went silent, and she sighed. "I never wanted to leave; I had to leave."

Nicole went on to explain that her father had had an episode. I always knew about his anger issues. Nicole would wear long-sleeved shirts to hide the bruising. That night was the pinnacle of the abuse; her mother was nearly beaten to death. When he passed out from his drunken stupor, she and her mother fled town.

The jovial atmosphere turned solemn as I processed the news. "I just wish you would have called me once you were finally settled. It really screwed me up, Nicole. For a very long time."

"I am really sorry, Eddie. I was young." She placed her hand on mine for a moment. "I was terrified he would find us. You know how quickly word spreads in this town."

We both stared out the window, watching heavy snowflakes fall from the heavens.

"I should go," Nicole said, snatching the bill before I could reach it.

"I'm sorry, Nicole. Stay for one more?"

She got up and paid the tab at the register. She chatted to David as he rang her in. He waved goodbye and dashed back behind the bar to tend to a stack of dirty mugs. When she returned, she had a troubled look on her face.

"I may be really out of line here, Eddie, but I would be kicking myself if I didn't at least try." She took a deep breath and handed me a folded napkin. "I wrote down my number and the address where I'll be staying tonight. I leave in the morning. But I would love for you to come by later?"

I shifted uncomfortably in my seat, as the magnitude of the offer settled in.

"You don't have to answer now—just give me a call later." She gave me a kiss on the cheek and left the bar.

And just like that, the snow leopard returned to the wild.

We had a late birthday dinner at Mckenzie's that evening. I was barely present for the festivities. Thoughts were racing through my mind from earlier at the bar. I couldn't help but imagine my life with Nicole if she had never left town. The chemistry was still there, I could feel it running electric through my veins. It was a feeling I had never felt with Karen, even at our best. I still loved her and the life we had built, but if I was being honest with myself, the two just weren't the same. It was an insane notion to have, our best years having passed us by. Had we been reunited in our twenties, circumstances could have been different. I had responsibilities now, bonds that had been forged from a lifetime of memories. The inner battle raged on for the rest of the evening.

When Karen began to cut the cake, I snuck out to the garage to make the call.

"Hello?"

"Hi Nicole, it's Eddie."

"Eddie! I'm so happy you called. I—"

"Listen, Nicole," I cut in, pausing a moment to articulate my thoughts. "It was lovely seeing you today. Really. But I don't think it's a good idea for me to come over." There was a long pause that I rushed to fill, "I really hope you understand. I have a family now, responsibilities. It's just not easy." I exhaled slowly. "That said, Nicole, next time you're in town, I would really love to grab another drink."

"But... I thought you wanted to rekindle what we had." Her heartache seeped through with every word.

"I never said that, Nicole. I was excited. I hadn't seen you in decades."

Another long, excruciating pause.

"Well, I'm really sorry to hear that, Eddie," Nicole said, through gentle sobs. "I'm an old fool. Forget this ever happened. I guess... I just hoped it was never too late for us."

"Nicole..."

Her tone shifted. "You know what? Maybe I'll stop by Mckenzie's tomorrow before I leave. Maybe I'll deliver a little belated birthday surprise. See what Chloe and Veronica think about their granddad seducing a former lover?"

Regret washed over me instantly. My heart raced rapidly in my chest, the pain forcing a hand to my left breast. "Listen—I don't know what you think happened here today, but I'm telling you it was nothing. Just two old friends running into each other. That's it. You hear me?"

"*Friends*?" she wailed, like I had thrust a dagger through her heart. "Well, I'll see you tomorrow then, 'friend'. Twenty-two Bridgestone Boulevard. Correct?"

My hands trembled. *How the hell did she know the address?*

"Nicole!"

She hung up, leaving me to marinate in the mess I had created. Before returning to the party, I made two more attempts at contact. Both calls went straight to voicemail.

⬡

I heard every creak that evening, every whistle of wind through the window, every siren off in the distance. I was wide awake, anticipating the doom that was soon to follow. There was a solid explanation to be had; I just couldn't prepare for the flurry of words that would spew out of Nicole's mouth. Her shift in demeanor was alarming. She seemed completely unpredictable. Nostalgia had seemingly washed away my recollection of the real her.

Karen spent most of the day with the grandchildren while Mckenzie went to work. She chased the kiddos around the yard and did finger painting with them all afternoon. I remained on edge, expecting Nicole to barge in at any moment to destroy everything I had ever worked for. All it took was one mistake. Her words wielded immense power, regardless of whether they were based in truth.

I waited nervously by the window for a visitor that never came. She didn't make an appearance until I turned on the evening news:

Good evening. This is KXB Channel nineteen—breaking news. In a scene right out of a movie, local county sheriffs arrested "The Black Widow Killer", Courtney Dolling. Wanted for the murders of former husbands: NYC entrepreneur David Dolling and career criminal Alonzo Herro, along with a slew of other charges including child trafficking and endangerment. She had been known to police for decades, going by a slew of different aliases. In an epic turn of events, she was identified by a local bartender and tracked down at a nearby Bakersfield hotel. A car chase ensued with police apprehending her in the early hours of the morning in a quiet residential area. The pursuit lasted upwards of an hour. More information is coming in by the minute as police begin to unravel the tale. Stay tuned.

The footage on the screen was of Nicole: her bulky coat did its best to shield her from the cameras. Although it was inaudible, her mouth moved frantically in wild, snarling contortions. There was a fire in her eyes that I didn't recognize: it was seething.

It was evil.

She was ushered away in handcuffs by police. The story left me stunned and suspended in my seat. Part of my heart hurt for her, but a much larger part was thoroughly relieved.

The snow leopard had been captured.

DOWN THE SPIRAL STAIRCASE

Alice hated the unknown. The technical term for her was "control freak". She always crossed every "T" and dotted every "I". There were no surprises in Alice's world. Yet, for some reason, she found herself here—dazed and confused and all alone.

What the fuck is going on?

This isn't like me, she thought. *Not like me... at all.*

She stumbled through the halls of the unknown lobby. The pot lights shone bright, almost blinding. She had never taken a drug in her life, hell, not even a sip of alcohol, but this is what she imagined the feeling to be like—delirious, disorientated, loopy.

Out of control, she gulped. Her worst nightmare now a reality.

Think, Alice. Think.

She rummaged through her memory banks for an inkling of what happened. There were no clues, just a foggy haze, and that terrified her to her core.

She wore her favorite yellow sundress and high-heel combo. There was a rainbow gift bag in her hand. *Clearly, I am on my way to celebrate something*, she thought. Or was she coming back from a party? A birthday? Maybe a housewarming? The not-knowing was excruciating.

As she attempted to trace back the memory, she noticed a fuzzy sound in the lobby. The halls were filled with inaudible chatter.

She reached for the bag and tried to open it. The opening was sealed shut, and a single folded note lay across the top. The note read "12th Floor" in permanent marker.

She bit her nails. It wasn't much to work off of, but at least it was something. Rather than tearing the gift bag apart, she decided to follow the instructions on the note.

The elevators were broken. A sign on the wall pointed directly to the stairwell. Her head pulsated as she followed the arrow, the room shaking from side to side in a sea-sick motion. Her stomach was aching too: twisted and hot like someone had ripped out her intestines and tossed them on the grill. Through all the pain, she still found herself at the foot of the stairs.

She started to climb the spiral staircase at a gingerly pace, the sound of her heels clacking against the pavement. The black metal railing was cool to the touch. It wobbled from side to side as her hand slid up the structure. The stairwell was quiet, only the echoes of her footsteps could be heard as she made her ascent. She made it to the first floor before she heard a familiar voice.

"*Alice*?" a woman shouted in a creaky tone.

As Alice wrapped around the corner, she saw it was her Nanna: one of her hands was holding the door to the hall ajar, the other holding her cat-eye style frames in place. She grinned from ear to ear. "Look at you, darling! Oh, my goodness... look how much you've grown!"

"*Nanna*?" Alice responded, one eyebrow raised.

"Come along, dear," she urged. "I've got some tea on the kettle waiting for you. Maybe some other treats if you behave." She waved for her to come closer. "Oh, my goodness, we have so much to talk about!"

The tantalizing smell of freshly baked apple pie carried into the stairwell. Alice's mouth began to water.

"*Ally*? Is that you?"

Gramps now accompanied Nanna at the doorway, strands of his silver hair were combed neatly across his forehead. He had a permanent frown across his face (wrinkles formed from a lifetime of grumpiness that he blamed on stupid politicians and underperforming sports teams), but the man was as gentle as they come. He was always sweeter than honey to his granddaughter, and she could tell by his tender tone that he was just as excited as his wife to see her.

"*Gramps?*" she called out nervously. A chill swept up her spine.

"Darling! It's great to see you. Come on in. Make yourself at home."

Alice wanted to go. She did. She felt it was criminal to turn down a slice of pie, especially one from Nanna. But she hesitated...

For one, the lights in the hall seemed to be turned off. She couldn't see anything past the open door.

For two, Nanna and Gramps were... flickering. It was subtle, but it was there. If she squinted hard enough, she could make out the short-circuiting.

For three, she hadn't tasted a slice of pie from Nanna in years, ever since she passed away when Alice was a little girl. Gramps passed away shortly after from the grief.

She stepped backward, slowly, her fear hiding behind a flimsy smile. "I love you, Nanna. Love you, Gramps. I just really have to go. I'll stop by after my party is over and come for a visit?" Her lips quivered as she pulled away.

"Alice, no!" Nanna shouted. "We've missed so much time. So many memories. Please stay and spend some time with your old grandparents. Please!"

"She ain't coming back, Dolores," Gramps grumbled. "It's time to come in, Alice. Now!" He lunged forward, his cane banging against the floor.

Alice turned and ran, a tear streaming down her cheek. She nearly slipped on the first step, if it wasn't for the railing. She climbed and climbed, not daring to look back until she put a couple of flights between them. When she felt safe, she stared down, hoping for one final glimpse.

The hall was empty. There was only the slamming of a door.

◆

The stairs were an infinite vortex, spiraling upwards and upwards to the ceiling. Alice felt a nagging pain in the bridges of her feet. Her face felt hot, her calves tired. She didn't know how much more of this she could handle, the twelfth floor still seemed miles away.

On floor six, she heard music. A soft jazz tune was playing in the background as the sound of muffled conversation flowed out into the hall.

Curiosity got the better of Alice, as she paused at the foot of the stairs. *Continue up or have a peek?*

Her feet were begging for a break. Her breathing began to normalize as she stood and let the gentle melody of the saxophone calm her nervous mind.

She politely approached the open door. To her surprise, there was no corridor behind it. The door led to what looked like the entrance of an art exhibition. The lively room was jam-packed with people in flowing gowns and clever blazers.

She stood at the doorway, marveling at the pieces on display: complicated abstract art with vibrant colors and geometric shapes.

"Alice?" A man with a mustard yellow beanie broke through a small crowd of people. His velvet blazer looked too tight, and his basketball sneakers looked like clown shoes.

"Peter!" she exclaimed, blinking in disbelief.

"What took you so long?" Peter asked. "People have been gawking at your piece all night. Flocking to it like flies to shit, Alice. I'm not kidding." He gestured towards a large painting in the far-right corner: an intricate piece with bright three-dimensional lines and points on a navy-blue canvas. From a distance, it looked like a stunning constellation in the night sky.

Alice asked sheepishly, "Peter, what is this? Where are we?" The piece looked like it was her style, but she hardly recognized it.

He shook his head and shot her a look that was both annoyance and intrigue. A look only Peter could conjure up.

"Alice—you need to snap out of it. And quick." He rubbed his palms together and grinned. "I think you may have made it big with this one."

An older lady in a black dress approached Peter and placed her hand on his shoulder. She said something to him in French and winked back at Alice. It suddenly became apparent that *everyone* was speaking French.

The lady nudged Peter, pulling at his arm. He craned his neck towards the crowd building around the constellation painting, whispering to Alice before he left, "I have to go. But now is not the time to be shy. Go start introducing yourself."

Goosebumps grew on Alice's arms. She suddenly felt cold. She knew she hadn't painted anything in years. Something was off with the gallery: it seemed foreign and incredibly far away from the little town where Alice had settled down. She waited awkwardly at the doorway, enthralled by the atmosphere of the event. Peter hadn't aged a day, and it appeared as if he had finally made it. It looked like she had somehow finally made it too.

Her heart fluttered with trepidation as she took a step forward into the gallery. Her foot bounced off an invisible barrier. Something kept her on the outside with a magnetic-like force. She was repelled a few more times as she watched the crowd clap for something, their backs to her, in awe of the painting.

Her painting.

And a structure twinkled off in the distance with flashing red and blue lights. Behind the floor to ceiling windows was the signature Parisian landmark that she often dreamt of; one she would likely never see in person. She blinked in utter disbelief.

Then a frigid whoosh of air hit her. The music died, the door shuddering. Alice jolted back, just in time before the door slammed shut. A white number six hung from the grey metal door that blocked her path.

She tried the knob one last time and left, deflated, toward the stairwell.

She was sick of walking.

The air felt heavier—thicker and colder with every step. The floors felt further and further apart, the incline steeper and steeper. When she finally made it to floor eleven, she would have cheered if she hadn't been so out of breath.

One more floor, she kept telling herself. *One more floor. One more floor.*

But floor twelve never seemed to come. It was spiral after endless spiral.

The stairs above looked like a swirling cyclone, taunting her from the sky. And Alice was trapped in the eye of the storm. Completely out of control.

She counted two hundred and eighteen steps before she finally gave up. She collapsed in exhaustion, curling up into a pathetic ball in the middle of the flight of stairs. The gift bag tumbled down, ten steps or so. The note floated down with it, slipping through a crack between the steps. She watched the bag eventually get stuck, trapped between the spokes of the metal railing wrapped around the corner.

A shrill cry escaped her throat. It was a helpless moan she couldn't contain. The tears followed closely behind as her cries echoed down the stairwell.

Amidst the bellowing, the lights went out.

Her body froze. The hair on her neck stood erect as she shuddered in confusion.

Silence, for a moment. Then the striking of a match.

A candle was lit on a vanilla frosted cake at the top of the stairs. Then another, and another, until a pretty little girl's face emerged from the shadows. She was just a toddler, her eyes beaming with wonder and excitement. A woman in black held her tight, only her chest level was visible. Another person held the cake up to the kid's face, waiting for her to blow out the candles. The little girl had a cute pink bow in her hair and wore a polka-dot dress.

Alice remained still, taking shallow breaths in apprehension. She waited in the darkness as others appeared in the candlelight behind the young girl. All she could see were their legs accompanied by loud shuffling.

The railing suddenly shook violently. Alice turned to see a feeble beam of light coming from a cheap LED flashlight (one of those pocket flashlights you can find at convenience stores). The light dropped, the flashlight rolling around the bottom flight below Alice.

"Alice, come get your gift," a raspy voice whispered in her ear.

She screamed, flinching in the pitch black. There was clapping coming from the top of the stairs.

Due to the angle of the light, she could only see the person's hip at the bottom of the stairs. The figure wore an orange reflective vest, dirt-stained jeans, and muddy steel-toe boots. The gift bag was now in the person's hand, lightly bouncing up and down in a jingling motion.

She hesitated, sandwiched between the two peculiar scenes on either side of the stairs.

"Alice, take it. It's yours," the voice whispered.

She decided to oblige for fear of what would happen if she didn't. She took a few cautious steps downward, the click-clack of her heels echoing through the stairwell.

There was singing coming from above. She could hear the off-key chorus as she inched closer to the light:

Happy birthday to you. Happy birthday to you.

Her hand trembled as she extended her arm. She clutched the string, and the figure let go of its grip. Once in her possession, the bottom of the bag ripped. A wave of thick, viscous blood poured out of the bottom, cascading and flowing down the flight of stairs.

The singing abruptly stopped. It was replaced by a shrill shriek that shook Alice's bones.

A force pushed her, knocking Alice against the cold, hard steps. She saw, for the last time, the beautiful spiral of metal that seemed to go on forever.

Suddenly everything went white.

◈

"Alice!"

She recognized her mom's voice, tears of joy dripping down her face. Alice was groggy and confused, but she finally felt safe. Her eyes darted across the room. She could see the various tubes attached to her body. It made her anxious, her heart beating in an erratic panic.

"Oh my God, she's awake! Hold tight, dear. I'll grab the doctor." Alice's mom dashed out of the room and re-entered accompanied by the medical staff. A lady in pale pink scrubs shined a light into Alice's eyes and performed a copious number of tests.

"Welcome back, Alice," the doctor said, warmly.

She told Alice to get some rest and left the room. Her mother, Janice, was looking rough—her hair disheveled and smelling of sweat.

"I left a voicemail with Warren. He's just at work, you know, finishing up those residential buildings on the east side of town. They're almost done now, Alice. Can you believe it? I feel like they've been in construction forever. Years in the making..." She smiled, placing her hand on Alice's arm. "I know once he hears the news, he's going to come running!"

Janice broke down in tears again, her voice trembling as she spoke, "No one believed you would wake up again, baby." She paused, blowing her nose into a tissue. "Not even your husband, God bless him. He'd never say it, of course, but I could see it in his eyes. But I did. You know me. I'm stubborn. You know me. I knew you would, love. I knew you would."

She rose from her seat and grabbed a tissue from the table. Beside the tissue box were various arrangements of flowers and teddy bears. Janice sniffled as she patted her eyes.

After a while, she wandered back to the chair next to Alice's bed. Alice could tell something more was on her mind. She had a dark, troublesome look across her face, an expression Alice dreaded seeing as a child.

Alice focused, using every ounce of energy to try to move. She managed to wearily place her palm on her mother's arm.

Janice's tepid smile turned into a look of concern. Alice stared into her eyes, the eyes of a woman who never gave up on her daughter.

"They told me to wait... to give you time to recover," Janice said. "But it's eating me up inside, Alice. It's been nothing but absolute torture." She contemplated a little longer before the words found their way out of her pursed lips in the form of a shaky whisper:

"You deserve to know, Alice. And sooner rather than later."

Alice tried to respond, but nothing came out. Her body tensed up as her mother continued.

"You've been in a coma for a year now, love. Twelve months, damn near right on the dot." She paused, searching for the right words. "You took a nasty tumble down the stairs of your apartment."

Janice tried to continue, but tears took over. She collapsed into her hands, and began to sob in an exhausted release of emotion. As Alice waited for Janice to continue, she struggled to validate the story she was hearing.

"You were out cold. The doctors tried their best..." She exhaled, patting the tears away.

"They rushed you to the operating room, dear. We were hopeful, despite it all. You were so close to the big day... But in the end, there was nothing they could do."

Alice could feel tears welling up in her eyes as she watched the sorrow exude from her mother.

"I'm so sorry, Alice," she swallowed.

"The baby, it couldn't be saved."

THE HAND OF THE DEVIL

After the initial devastation, after all the tears were shed, panic starts to settle in. My mind rolls through the various options.

I'm thinking of the circular saw. I picture it lying there in the top drawer of the cabinet, a tool purchased on a whim, still with its new plastic smell. Sixty carbide-tipped blades with teeth that could rip through sheet metal. All it would take is one straight cut—clean, simple—right across the joint in order to avoid chiseling away at the bone.

Either that or the hacksaw would do the trick. It would be messy, but it would be over.

Tools in the dusty drawers of my garage—this is where my troubled mind was settling. Practicality. Organization. I guess in times of trauma you revert back to who you are.

The screaming has stopped, but the prevailing silence has proven to be much worse. Its emptiness provides opportunity; my mind begins to linger in the dark recesses of its confines. Trudging to the corners you avoid, the places you never want to be.

The room looks like a hurricane has run through it: pillows, bedsheets, glasses, and the remains of an overturned lamp all litter the floor. I pick up shards of glass from the picture frame that tumbled from the wall. Stacy and the finest version of myself are staring back at me through the photo. I'm in a tuxedo on the beach, she's in her strapless wedding dress. The flowing lace contoured to her body is breathtaking, the train flares out in a wave of white across the sand. I'm thirty pounds lighter in the photo. Stacy is sporting a genuine smile.

This is all before the accident, the one that left me in a coma and out of work for nearly a year. All I remember were the head-lights before waking up in the hospital. The rehab was a long and arduous process, learning to walk and talk again like a child. Stacy was my caretaker through it all, she did everything for me. And although this was years ago, I still feel like this is the point where it all began to crumble.

And now my mind wanders to the inevitable, the impossible predicament of it all. The thought of it brings me to my knees.

The tragedy of what's just happened and how to plausibly explain it. People think the truth is always the answer; I used to be this naive. If you have nothing to hide, then why cower behind a fictitious account of events? But the *honest* truth is that an accurate account of events is only acceptable if someone else is willing to believe the facts. Regardless of how certain situations unfold, some events lack logic.

Some things just can't be explained.

And I knew that the truth just wouldn't cut it here; I needed a better story, and fast.

The shards of glass slip off the scooper and land in the garbage. I pace around the bedroom. After a while, the plan hits me:

A disappearance.

She simply vanished into thin air. Skipped town with some guy she met on our vacation to Cuba last winter.

I sigh. The explanation feels paper-thin, but it will have to do. It was the only one I had.

I stumble as I step over her, my eyes bloodshot and stinging. I tuck the corner of the bed sheets in, tight. The pillows plop back into place as if nothing ever happened. The last bit of clutter is erased. I lug her suitcase from the closet, and just as I wheel it to the other side of the bed, something collides with my big toe. It slides smoothly across the hardwood floor. I crouch under the bed and flinch as our eyes meet. She looks empty as she stares back at me, her left cheek flat to the floor.

It's that same stare she gave me when she found out that *I* was the one who crossed the median that fateful night. *I* was the one who had been drinking. *I* was the one trying to die, but instead, God chose to take the family in the minivan.

I force my eyes shut. The room is quiet, but there is a faint muffle coming from the other end of the bed. I army crawl closer to the headboard, towards the tiny beacon of light. I extend my arm across the floor, flakes of dust floating all around me. Stacy watches as I grasp the object.

It's her Blackberry. The outgoing call to 9-11 is still active.

I slither out from under the bed and rise to my feet. I disconnect the call before chucking the phone against the wall.

My fist follows—a web of cracks spreading from the dent in the drywall.

Pain shoots up my right arm.

Everything blurs as I grab Stacy by her ankle. I manage to drag her a few inches, but her limp body is too heavy, and the pain is now too much. I run down the stairs, my arm banging wildly against the railing, fighting with me the whole way down.

The garage is cold and dark, but I manage to paw at the light switch. I make it to the toolbox, just as I hear the sirens blaring through the neighborhood. The neighbors will be on their front lawns in a matter of seconds. Time has officially run out.

And now the true story unfolds.

The flailing—wild, violent, uncontrollable jerks—has become overwhelming. It seems to have been triggered by the panic and the screeching sirens. My left arm swings in the air and pounds my chest in a reckless pattern of chaos.

But you can hardly call it *mine,* anymore.

This hand that I no longer recognize has escaped the confines of my makeshift cast. The feeble jail cell that I constructed out of knotted bed sheets is still partially strung across my body. The flimsy construction job was not enough, and now my wife is gone forever.

No one listened when I told them—not the doctors, not Stacy. I begged someone to do something, that this numbness was not normal. But all I received were some pain meds and a recommendation for a physiotherapist—the *best* physiotherapist in the city.

Now the phantom limb with a mind of its own is now free. My right arm severely compromised, my left arm full of bloodlust.

The one that wrapped its fingers around my wife's throat, squeezing the life out of her lungs in her sleep, it seems to have awoken again and caught a second wind.

I hear the sirens outside on the drive pad. I can see the beams of a flashlight through the window.

I now realize I will have to compromise.

I take a few steps toward the opposite wall, peering out the window that sits above the tool cabinet. I grab the hammer hanging from a nail in the drywall. I side-step past the bike rack.

There is no time to amputate, but maybe I can find the strength to bash it to a pulp. I glance out of the corner of my eye at the erratic limb, the fingers are flaring in and out in an unpredictable manner. There are deep scrapes and bruising all along the forearm, war wounds inflicted by both Stacy and myself.

Mid-swing, I see my left-hand flash toward the weapon. We battle for control as I wince from the pain.

Police! Open the door!

I hear them in the hallway. I scream, "Shoot me! I'm in the garage!" The pain in my right arm is excruciating, the throbbing brings tears to my eyes. Both arms wrestle for an edge.

Shaky apologies escape from my throat. Warnings follow, but the words come out a blubbering mess.

I hear footsteps approaching the door. My left hand sways above my head, triumphantly gripping the hammer.

The door catapults open, just as I manage to articulate the whimpers into words:

"I'm sorry officers."

And the devil swings.

LIFELINE DENIED

There was the voice before there was anything. It bellowed with a strength that could part seas and move mountains. *TAKE YOUR SEAT.*

My eyes opened to reveal the presence of a crowd. People flooded into the room: shuffling into the empty pews and plopping themselves into seats. Past the railing, on the other side of a gated barrier, I sat atop a small platform that faced the crowd. From this vantage point, I could see everything. The horde of people was quickly subsiding: most had claimed a seat at the pews while a small group was ushered past the metal gates and were seated near the corner of the room. No matter where they were located, their gaze was fixed on one target. I felt the eyes of a hundred people, maybe more, upon me.

The chatter died down into a whisper when the people with briefcases entered the room. A woman with a tight bun and tighter slacks flashed her credentials. She was permitted entry past the gates. Gravitating to a nearby table, she was accompanied by a stubby man with glasses.

The odd duo did very little in the way of acknowledging one another. They were busy extracting documents and notebooks out of their bags and organizing the bundles of paper into piles. An identical process was occurring at the table to the right of them. Two men who looked like they could be brothers—their thick manes of ebony curled in a similar, well-groomed fashion—were reaching into their saddlebags and pulling out ungodly amounts of paper.

QUIET.

The whispers ceased.

LET US BEGIN.

The gazes shifted from my direction to the peculiar couple at the table; the lady and the compact man whispered to each other for a moment. She eventually departed from the table with a piece of paper in her hand.

"Thank you all for joining us today. It's never easy to be a part of these proceedings." She stifled a cough as she scanned the room. "My name is Jamie Leeward." She paused, pointing to the short man at the table. "And this is my associate, Peter Briggly. Together—we are here to represent Mason Meadows."

The lady's delivery was crisp, her movements confident and calculated. She was now beside me on the platform, staring into my eyes.

"We believe he deserves to live..."

My heart pumped violently in my chest when I realized I couldn't move. I tried to address Jamie for clarification, but nothing came out. The failed attempts continued—no matter how hard I tried to concentrate or how hard I strained to speak—access to my faculties was restricted. My responses were muted; I was disconnected from both my body and my memories.

"... and over the course of this proceeding, we believe you will too." Darkness fell over the room, accompanied by the sound of shuffling paper. Something in my brain had shifted. The feeling was subtle, like the birth of a new idea or catching a word on the tip of your tongue. The synapses fired up to produce a memory in the form of a hologram. My mind materialized the moment into beams of light that were projected from my eyes toward the center of the room.

"Let us start at the beginning."

A sudden barrage of memories flooded my system. They bottlenecked in my brain, slowly playing one by one, scene by scene, like a film reel. Each memory on display felt as fresh and as vivid as the first time I'd experienced it. Highlights of my childhood were playing for the crowd: snowball fights in the dead of winter with my brother, camping trips spent with the family huddled by the fire. Pivotal moments—like the first time I learned how to ride a bike—were sprinkled in with seemingly insignificant moments in time: silly laughter fits at the dinner table and cozy movie nights on the sofa. They all played, one by one, in a cleverly edited production.

"On the surface, Mason looks like he had a happy childhood." Jamie let the memories play, allowing the audience to soak it all in. The reel painted a beautiful picture of a loving family and cheerful child. She continued, "Below the surface, however, it was anything but that. This young man: Mason Meadows, the eldest child. He never had much of a chance."

Peter Briggly took the stage and began his deliberation. "You see, things were mostly good for Mason when he was tending to the farm, finishing up his homework, and eating all of his fruits and vegetables. You know, being a good boy and all. The problem was Mason wasn't always a good boy, as most boys aren't." As he slowly approached the group seated in the corner, I felt the fibers in my brain beginning to fire up.

The memory exited my eyeholes: I saw the steep mahogany stairs leading us below, into the darkness. I knew exactly where we were going: it was a trip down to the cool room, a place I knew far too well. Father had a fistful of my hair as I groveled for forgiveness.

"Handsss on the waaallll, Mayce!" Father slurred. "Take your lickin's like a man."

Down came the leather belt, the strap whipping at a menacing pace. Again—slicing into my back. Purple welts began to form around trickles of blood.

"When will you learn? When?"

My whimpers did nothing to wipe the grimace from his face.

"Next time you cut the GOD – *whip* – DAMN – *whip* – GRASS – *whip* – when I ask. You hear me?"

Stop! I screamed at Peter. *Turn it off*! The words remained trapped inside my conscious mind. I sat alone with my cries for help, the crowd's gaze glued to the hologram playing. The beating continued.

I knew this moment (I had lived through it, of course) but experiencing it again in front of others felt like swallowing a gallon of poison. The crowd seemed to share in my sentiments; their faces contorted in displeasure. But no one looked away.

"Mason has ten years of trips down to the cool room. I could keep these memories going for hours. Imagine the accumulation of trauma." Peter shook his head. "This is suffering. And all we ask the council, no, we *beg* the council to please consider the effects of this on a child's mind. Mason is not his father. Right now, it is all he knows. But separated from this monster, we believe he has real potential to do good in this world. Don't let this boy go to waste."

"Bullshit!" shouted a pudgy lady in the front.

More disgruntled bickering came from the back of the room.

A middle-aged man in the back was playing a tiny violin with his hands.

QUIET.

The resounding voice shook the crowd into silence.

WHAT WAS HIS TRAJECTORY?

Jamie skimmed through one of the stacks of papers. She chimed in from the table, "His metrics were very promising. You can have a look for yourself." She proceeded to hand documents to each member of the council as she continued, "High IQ. Suitable values. Malleable temperament. Apart from the obvious, he was a rattled and confused child. It will take some time. But with proper resources, we believe he has a high probability of becoming a contributing member of society. Overall, his charts suggest upwards."

THANK YOU BOTH.

Peter nodded, following Jamie back to the table.

One of the curly-haired men took his cue and stepped toward the middle of the room. His suit had a waxy sheen that seemed to sparkle in the light emitted from the hologram. "Mason's case is a tragic case. A broken home. A turbulent childhood." He turned to the council, all of their weathered faces turning to him, "You've all been around long enough to have seen cases like his before."

Some people in the crowd shifted in their seats.

"I don't say that to discount Mason's experiences. The kid went through a lot in his fifteen years. I say that to warn you not to be swayed by the touching backstory that has been presented to you today. That is *not* how this process is supposed to work."

He turned to me, as I felt my memory bank being tapped into once again.

The beams of light emanating from my eyes began to play another memory.

"My name is Stu Tallow." He paused, motioning to the table behind him, "And this is Marcus Brent. We represent the best interests of the Order."

I braced myself as the memory materialized for the crowd. We were transported to the confines of the hay barn at my parent's farm. I was playing with the boy from up the road, Chuck. We were bored and goofing off, grabbing each other and wrestling around the bales of hay. He was much older than I was, but given the lack of kids in our town, we hung out with whoever was around. During a tripping match, Chuck managed to pin me to the floor. We were both cackling like hyenas as I bucked to try to get him off. He stared into my eyes. We were a mess—hay strands sprinkled all over our heads and bodies. The game stopped, for a moment, before he leaned in. Our lips touched. The gesture confused me, but in a swift jerk, I was pulled in closer. He kissed me again, the pillars of dried grass keeping our bodies hidden. At least that's what I thought, until I heard snickering.

It was coming from the top of the loft. My brother Daylan's face peered down from the wooden railing. A smile stretched across his face.

"Maycey—grooosssss."

I dashed for the ladder and pulled myself up, rung by rung. The little menace was weaving in and out of sight, disappearing behind the yellow towers of hay.

"I'm telling Dad! I'm telling Dad!" he laughed. Treacherous little giggles.

I knew if this ever got to my father, there were worse consequences than the belt.

"Daylan. Stop. For a damn second—please!" He wouldn't listen.

I managed to corner him along the perimeter. He tried his best to cut around me, but I swiped at him at full speed. My arm collided with his shoulder, spinning him off his center of gravity. He teetered on the edge of the loft. His eyes went wide, his arms swinging in an effort to correct his balance. He dropped with a thud that made the chickens stir in their coop.

A gasp came from the crowd.

"There was no intent," Peter argued.

"Oh, bullshit," Marcus retorted. "And how would you know that?"

I felt naked. My mind filleted and spread wide open for these strangers to peek inside. They judged. They gawked. Some dusty men in the front shook their heads in disapproval.

They didn't understand how much I loved my brother or how much I feared my father. If I could cry, the tears would have flowed in a steady stream. Instead, I sat in silence with an aching heart.

Stu spoke, "Regardless of what you believe or don't believe, the facts still remain. Mason Meadows took a life." The reel kept playing as Stu continued, "His brother, Daylan, was only six years old."

My distraught self slung Daylan's body over my shoulder. Draped over me like a blanket, his lifeless limbs swayed from side to side. Blood leaked from the fracture in his skull.

Chuck must have fled during the commotion. The only two who remained were me and what used to be my brother.

I trudged out of the barn wearing the shame across my face. The magnitude of my actions settled in as the sun dropped behind the hills.

Father would be home soon.

I choked back my tears, the agony twisting my innards in knots. I knew I needed a plan. An explanation. I searched for one aimlessly in the twilight.

When it hit me like a lightning strike, I darted toward the vehicle, the dead weight of Daylan slumped over me.

Father's Chevy Silverado. The keys were still in the ignition.

His baby purred, the Hemi roaring with more horsepower than he could ever use. I shifted the truck into drive, my hands trembling as I gripped the wheel. I took the route around the back, down the dirt road that led past the cornfields. The floodlights guided me through the prevailing darkness.

Once we made it past the fields, I took one last look at Daylan, his lifeless body lying in the front seat.

I stomped on the gas, the truck accelerating at a reckless clip. We sailed straight into the middle of the pond, the beastly tires spinning viciously, kicking up frenetic waves. My shrieks were swallowed up by the rising water. Bubbles trickled to the surface. I watched my brother's body float to the roof of the truck. Then the memory faded out and the broadcast disappeared.

The room was filled with silence as the lights switched on.

"Council," Stu pleaded, stepping closer to the group of elders. "We get thousands of these occurrences every day. A perfect place, a perfect time. A tiny window of opportunity." He turned and scowled in my direction. "This_boy not only murdered his brother, but he also took his own life. He's demonstrated zero regard for existence. Why would we grant someone like this a lifeline over all of the other candidates?"

"Bullshit, Stu," Jamie retorted. "The metrics are why!"

"With all due respect," Marcus shouted, "we interpret the numbers differently." He cleared his throat as the air in the room thickened. "Low EQ. Childhood trauma. This is far from a slam dunk; there are many variables to consider. I agree with Stu. I urge the council to consider some of the other candidates this evening."

In the background, the crowd engaged in debates amongst themselves. "Send him away!" a stocky man bickered. "On to the next!"

COUNCIL: PLEASE CONSIDER.

One by one, the group of elders left their seats and walked through a back door. They were gone for what seemed like an eternity, the time dragging on within the confines of the dull beige walls. Amongst the quiet conversations, I recognized a familiar face in the crowd. Grandma was chatting off the ear of a finely-dressed gentleman. Her cheeks had the same rosy glow that I often missed.

The fate of my soul wavered in the air of this stuffy little room, somewhere between life and death.

Then the door swung open; one by one the councilmen and women claimed their seats, all of them donning expressions of stone.

HAS THE COUNCIL COME TO A DECISION?

"We have," a lady with silver hair announced. "After careful consideration, the vote was close. But we are in favor of granting Mason Meadows a lifeline. Five votes to four."

The crowd grumbled. A few people in the back threw their hands up in frustration.

I held my breath, scanning the room for a clue as to what would happen next. Jamie and Peter were trading whispers, patting each other on the back. Stu and Marcus tried their best to suppress their stunned expressions. No one left their seats.

The room waited in anticipation, my soul wavering a little longer. Then the voice spoke with a definitiveness akin to the banging of a gavel.

LIFELINE—DENIED.

The crowd erupted in hysteria. A trump card had been played. Or maybe a split vote went to the Order. Either way, Jamie and Peter looked livid as they approached members of the council. Their complaints were drowned out by cheering; the people would not go unheard.

It was clear the opportunity for a miracle had come and gone. The near-death experience had turned into death.

A man in black ushered the four presenters and the council out the back door. He left only me on the other side of the fence as the locking mechanism clicked open. The crowd stormed the gates, funneling through the entryway. Their eyes were different now: gleaming, blood-red, and ravenous. No longer contained, they sprinted in my direction and pulled my body to the floor. I screamed a desperate shriek that only I could hear. Grandma sunk her teeth into my throat, a bloody grin across her face. The others ripped me limb from limb, whatever piece they could get their hands on.

Justice had been served.

⬢

A layer of mist rose from the pond as I watched my father's Silverado sink deeper and deeper. Only the roof of the truck remained visible.

His baby—drowned in the water. He would never recover from that. I figured he might miss Daylan and myself too.

I was nothing more than a silhouette, a shadow walking the dirt road carved into the thick crops. I walked through the pitch-black accompanied by the sounds of nature: frogs and crickets singing tunes with fervor.

It was a long walk back to the house.

I had nothing to go back to; my opportunity had come and gone. My body was floating in the pond somewhere, likely at the bottom of it now. I wasn't upset with the decision: it wasn't something I expected, and it wasn't something I deserved. I was never good at life, anyways. I struggled to navigate the world.

There were endless opportunities for me now. I had found a new purpose.

Father would finally know what it felt like to live in fear.

PERRY

Sometimes people walk into your life that stay with you forever.

Before Perry, I was a fish out of water. A little guppy, from a small town, looking for a fresh start in the city. Like most town_folk, I put city life on a pedestal. I dreamt about all of the opportunities that this new move would bring. Deep down, I knew I was running. Running as far away as I could from my former sheltered life, one that my parents tried to control with a loving, but overbearing, grasp.

The loneliness hit me like a stack of bricks those first couple of weeks. I learned how socially anxious I truly was without my safety net of childhood friends. Still, I smiled. I introduced myself. I did all of the bullshit that self-help gurus tell you about breaking out of your comfort zone. I tried to stick behind at work functions and join as many rec sports teams as I could.

The thing about breaking out of your comfort zone is that it's uncomfortable as shit. I wasn't used to being a nobody. People had their own established social circles built up from years of shared experiences. They weren't exactly looking to add a shy country girl into the mix.

So, it was just me, for a while, trying to adjust to the bright lights of the big city.

This dream life had become one big monotonous routine. Tuesday night was reserved for *"The Bachelor"*. Wednesday night was for hot yoga. And the day I lived for most, Friday, was typically spent on the couch with a bottle of Merlot.

On a good week, I might have had a date lined up for the weekend. Some guy who'd message me on Tinder, we would agree to meet up at a sports bar downtown and end up splitting the bill. Staring across the table at Mr. Tinder, it's like you are viewing him from a funhouse mirror. Elements of him are the same, he's not a total fraud. But his belly in that button-up shirt is a little rounder, his toothy smile just a little more crooked. The personality that sealed the deal—his witty remarks and quips through text—don't seem to hit the same when delivered through his nasally tone. I imagine he sees me through his own distorted mirror, too.

So, it was just me, for a while longer.

Until Perry showed up at my door on a Sunday evening. This was my designated day of dread, awaiting another mind-numbing work week. I had just given up on a row of leftover expired sashimi for dinner. Spitting out the gob of mush (whatever remnants I hadn't already consumed), I apprehensively made my way to the door.

A bean-stalk of a man smiled through the peephole. His head was shaved and a clipboard was clutched to his chest.

"Good evening, ma'am. Sorry to bother you. I'm with TelSat Services. I was wondering if I could speak with you for a moment? Are you satisfied with your current cable provider?"

I told him I was, but he was persistent.

"If I could steal ten minutes of your time, I'll show you what you're missing out on."

He laid out a brochure that included a plethora of bundled TV channel packages: hundreds of combinations of on-demand movies and twenty-four-hour cooking shows.

I told him I didn't even know what a soufflé was, but he was persistent.

There wasn't enough hours in the day to watch all of the television he was pushing. Regardless, by the time he left, I was a brand new TelSat customer. Forty new channels, three cooking networks, and a couple of channels in Cantonese.

And he walked away with my number.

If I'm being honest, at first, I didn't give him much of a chance. He wasn't handsome by any of the traditional metrics. His neck stretched long like a goose. His skin was so translucent you could make out the green-blue veins on his forehead. But as time went on, he began to grow on me. I decided to give him a chance. What he lacked in looks, he more than made up for in personality. He was confident, he was devoted. He was a lot of things I wasn't, and at the worst of times, he was an absolute pillar of support.

However, the more time I spent with him, the more I began to notice something alarming. His body seemed to be getting frailer. Every day he looked less human and more like a skin-stretched coat rack. This deterioration terrified me, as he didn't have much meat on his bones to begin with.

When I tried to question him, he'd push me away.

"Bug off, Tessa. Everything's fine."

I was beginning to sound like my parents. So, I shrugged it off too.

At this point, we were bonded. We were one of those couples that people gave dirty looks to as they made out in front of them in line. We were the couple they would make snide comments about under their breath.

Get a room! they'd mutter.

We'd laugh because we knew. We knew we were the couple they secretly wanted to be, or even worse, the couple they *used* to be. Our hands were one, cemented together, as we paraded around our love.

One night Perry took me to a *real* sushi restaurant. One of those places that doesn't serve food, they serve "art". You had to make a reservation months in advance in order to get into a place like that.

We sat in our secluded corner for hours talking about our future. Perry never had much of a family growing up, so it was important for him to build one. We looked on patiently as the chef wrapped every individual roll in front of us. We laughed at the pretentiousness of it all. I adored his geeky chortle.

Then I drove us home as fast as I could, Perry stroking my thigh all the way home. He led me to the bedroom, whispering softly:

"You're the one, Tessa."

The lights flicked off.

"You're the one."

My Japanese denim unzipped, falling to the floor.

"*Gosh,* you're the one."

He pushed me to the bed in a ravenous heat. His hands were silky-smooth as he caressed me in the darkness. I could feel him slowly burrowing deeper and deeper inside of me. And then faster, as I squirmed, riding waves of pure euphoria. My body jolted uncontrollably in spastic little bursts. It was pain and pleasure and pleasure and pain. My toes curled and flexed, digging deeper into the mattress. When I couldn't take it anymore, I moaned so loud the headboards shook. And then it was over. I could finally breathe.

I gathered my composure as the high faded.

"Perry, that was *amazing,*" I said, my head collapsing into the pillow.

No response.

"Perry?"

I turned on the lamp. The room was empty.

"Perry?"

Only silence and the stench of sex.

I freaked the fuck out, searching everywhere, calling out Perry's name. When it was clear he was gone, I made sure the doors were locked. Lying in my bed, staring hopelessly at the ceiling, the covers pulled close up to my face, I tried to imagine skinny Perry, buck-naked and barefoot, trotting home.

I wondered what I did wrong.

◆

There are still no signs of Perry. No one has seen him. No one has heard from him.

My mom calls, and I let it go to voicemail. This is the overbearingness that I talk about. She has always had these concerns and her worrying only makes me sicker.

Perry's left me in a gaping hole of anxiety and depression. The frustration, the not-knowing, these feelings wriggle around inside of me. I don't know what to do.

I've been filling the void he's left with food, ordering takeout from our favorite spots. My living room has become a landfill of pizza boxes and plastic containers. I have become a part of the filth; the dump is my new home.

I stuff my face with deep-crust pizza, pasta al-forno, and tightly-wound Mona Lisa sushi rolls. I believe the taste and the aromas help bring back the memories of us. But, really, I have no control.

My once curvaceous body is now a flesh bag of skin and bones. Nothing sticks, despite the cravings. So I keep feeding and feeding. I'm paler than he ever was now, a snow-storm blizzard white.

I'm slumped over on the sofa, waiting. For either him to return or the stress to eat me alive.

The not-knowing is the hardest part. It's drained every ounce of energy out of me. Things I used to love—volunteering, reading, and going to the gym—just don't seem to matter anymore.

But I am grateful for the TV package. I am confident I could become either a chef or a Chinese translator if I could ever get off of the couch.

The frightening part is that I can still feel him. His voice never goes away. I hear his whispers late at night, when the world is still. I hear his chortle, his words of endearment.

Just now, I hear him whisper:

"Tessa, you need to find your one."

For a moment, the throbbing in my abdomen subsides; the pain in my heart lessens.

I am terrified of what the future holds. I can't imagine doing anything without him.

Through a cheek full of rice and soy sauce, my bony arm reaches for the end table.

I fire up the old dating app and start swiping.

Searching for my one.

Our one.

JIMMY AND THE FLOWER BUG

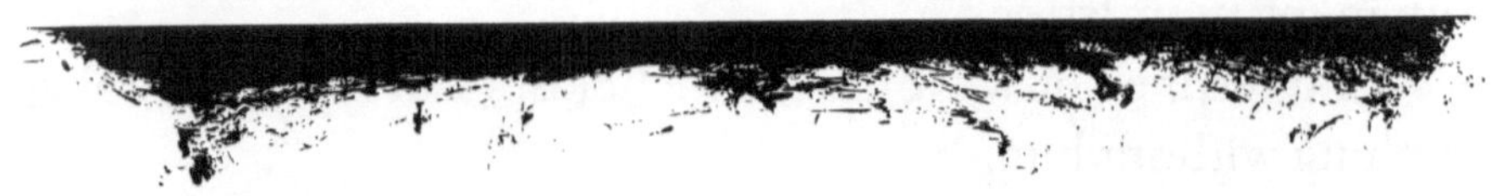

I read something today that reminded me of Jimmy. I'll admit, it had been years since the kid had crossed my mind. I sat at the kitchen table, staring out at the tangerine sky. It was early: the smell of poached eggs and brewed coffee filled the air. The house was still, my family quietly lying in bed. Everything was calm, almost peaceful. So why was my stomach twisted in knots?

Jimmy was a chubby child, the byproduct of a house that served sugar as a well-balanced diet. He waddled around the playground, his unflattering rolls popping out of unexpected places. He wasn't the nicest or the brightest kid, and he *definitely* wasn't the prettiest, but what he was, was an absolute force. A titan on the playground. He knew how to command respect and how to throw his weight around. He stood a foot taller than his classmates; kids cowered in his presence. That was the power of Big Jimmy Burke.

I won't pretend that our friendship was perfect. We had our fair share of ups and downs. Early on, I got too close. I opened myself up, and he wasn't ready. I played too close to fire and suffered the consequences.

Now, as an adult, I walked around the world concealing those scars: third-degree burns that never seemed to heal. I feel like we all do. We try our best to hide the pain, but the damage is still there.

I remember the time he pantsed me in gym class: my shorts, underwear, and pride all tossed on the linoleum floor.

Another time he dunked my head in the toilet for not laughing hard enough at one of his jokes. One of those chicken-crossing-the-road variations you've heard a million times.

It was hard to get close to Jimmy. He tried his best to test you, to push you away, and like a little whimpering dog, I always came back. I was loyal, for some reason, to Jimmy. Maybe it was because of the power he wielded; maybe because he gave me just enough attention, threw me just enough scraps every now and then.

Mainly, I think it was because I was afraid. School can be a cruel place for someone who is alone.

Those were the bad memories of Jimmy. The ones I buried away, deep.

No, the memory that had resurfaced this morning was a good one. It was his ninth birthday party, and I was waiting on his porch dressed in a Spiderman outfit. I remember the feeling of the tight spandex and the excitement of the occasion. There was a welcoming stench of cigarettes as the door opened. His mom and dad waved goodbye to mine.

Jimmy was the Hulk: shirtless with every inch of his body painted green. His fat jiggled as he grabbed his gift bag from me. "Landon's here, everybody! Landon's here! Let's start the party!"

Our crew was a tornado, wreaking havoc across the main floor of the home, pushing around toy cars and jumping on sofas. There were pit stops to throw cake down our gullets (with the occasional chunks flung at each other); but for the most part, we were left to bounce off the walls. Jimmy's mom was preoccupied with the phone, smoking a cigarette at the kitchen table. His dad was nowhere to be found, likely hiding from the chaos.

In the middle of a nerf gun shootout, Jimmy put a finger to his mouth.

"*Shhh.*"

Everyone shut up.

You could hear the rumble of a motor... the garage door slowly closing. "He's gone," Jimmy announced. "You guys wanna see something cool?"

We all nodded.

"Then be quiet, and come with me."

We tiptoed up the staircase, five miniature superheroes on a mission. We followed with bated breath as he led us to a locked door. Stuck on the door was a poster of a rock band I didn't recognize. The words "DO NOT ENTER" was scribbled in a bloody text along the top.

Thinking for a moment, he disappeared into his parent's bedroom. He returned with a hairpin to fiddle with the lock.

click

The door gave way to a messy, ill-lit room. The walls were painted black and plastered with posters of monsters and gothic rock bands. Everyone's jaw dropped when they saw the glass tanks, all stacked along the walls. In a trance, we stepped over the piles of clothing on the floor, toward the humming red heat lamps and buzzing motors. Inside was a collection of creatures that I had never seen before.

I pressed my hand against the cold glass, marveling at the bright colors. "What is that, Jimmy?"

He smiled. "That's a serpent starfish," he said, pointing at the thing with tentacles draped across a rock. "And those are Angelfish. And right there are Blenny's." He pointed to a vibrant school of fish, all swimming together in unison.

A resounding "*wow*" came from the room. We slowly gravitated from one tank to the next, wide-eyed in wonder.

Jimmy continued the tour: "Fire Belly Newt, Boa Constrictor, Red-Eyed Tree Frog." One by one, he pointed, and we oohed and awed.

I stopped while Jimmy led the others to new, unexplored areas of the bedroom. A small tank near the corner had caught my eye. The inside looked like a rainforest, but there were stunning pink flowers along one of the stumps. One of the flowers... was moving, in a slow, hypnotic fashion.

"Jimmy! What's this one?" I shouted.

The group stopped for a moment, and then dashed back toward me. Jimmy followed closely behind. The other kids crouched around me to get a better look.

"Oh, that's a good one there, Landy." Jimmy tapped his finger against the tank. "That right there is a flower bug."

"A flower bug?"

"Yup. Ain't it pretty?"

I couldn't keep my eyes off of it—the beautiful mix of white and fuchsia, its powerful pincers, its alien eyes.

The rest of the kids eventually lost interest and bolted out of the room. Not me. I lingered, marveling at the insect. I only stopped when I heard the door creak shut. The room got dark.

"You wanna see something *really* cool?" Jimmy asked, a faint whisper in the dark.

My heart galloped in my chest. " Sure! What is it?"

He turned on a flashlight and inched closer. "Then you gotta do something for me, first. And don't tell anyone about what I'm about to do. Ever."

I nodded, watching Jimmy maneuver in the dark.

In my teens, I worked at a pizza shop called Giovanni's Pies: the cheesiest, greasiest pizzas in the city. It was my first job as a lazy, inexperienced youth. So, you can imagine the type of responsibilities Giovanni had bestowed upon me: wiping the counters, prepping the pizzas, sweeping the floors, scrubbing the toilets.

Just make sure you ain't never step outta line or burn the damn place down or nuttin', he'd warn. *Or it's your ass or your paycheck. Y'a hear me?*

The pay could have been better, but you could do the job with your eyes closed. The only real problem was the hours: some nights we'd be on the clock till well after 2:00am. Fulfilling the cravings of the degenerate party crowd seemed to really matter to Giovanni. But when you're young, you bounce back from lack of sleep like a trampoline. Now, I can't even imagine how I survived with so little for all those years.

One night after a week of graveyard shifts, my coworker Will and I were closing up shop. It was a nasty winter night with a wind that cut through bone and whistled through the cracks in the window casing. I waved goodnight to Will, locked the door, and made sure the security cameras were running. He ran into the warmth of his mother's mini-van and drove away.

I walked across the empty parking lot toward my lonely station wagon. The wind was brisker than usual that evening—piercing and brutal. The fierce gusts shocked my system the second I left the restaurant. I picked up the pace, walking through the tornado of snow swirling around the lot. I hopped into the front seat and started the ignition.

Out of the corner of my eye, I saw something. A person—old, pudgy, Eastern European. The lady stared back at me from the passenger seat.

"What the hell are you doing? Get out of my car!" I screamed.

She recoiled, "Oy! I'm so sorry!" She broke down in tears, her voice shaking. "Have you seen my son, Mikeal? I thought this was his car."

"I don't know who the hell that is, lady. Now get out!"

She grabbed a handkerchief from her purse and wiped her eyes. "Oy! I'm so sorry. I will leave. I just don't know what to do. My son, Mikael, was supposed to get me from the pharmacy hours ago." She opened the passenger door, wincing at the howling wind. "Everything is closed. This door was open. Oy! I'm so sorry."

I took a moment to calm my nerves.

I did have a bad habit of forgetting to manually lock the doors in the old wagon. It was creepy, but the frigid temperature would have forced anyone to find shelter or risk freezing to death in the storm.

Just before she waddled away, I yelled for her to return.

She stared back at me, shivering. Her headscarf was pulled tight over her head, but it was thinner than a piece of paper. She had a solid build: her shoulders broad, her back hunched over like a camel's back.

"Can you give Mikael a call?" I asked.

She shook her head. "No phone."

I reached into my pocket. "Ah, okay... come back in. Shut the door." She rubbed her large gloves together and graciously repeated thanks. "What is his number?"

She rattled off a series of numbers. The call rang a few times and then went to voicemail. The recording said: "Hi, this is Erin. Leave me a message at the beep."

I hung up. "I don't think that's the right one."

She paused. "Oy. I'm losing all my marbles. It's *3354*, not 3534."

I rang the new number this time. Still no luck. This time the number wasn't registered to anyone.

"Ma'am, I'm going to need you to really think here. Try your best to remember..."

She let out a deep, apologetic sigh. "I'm sorry, dear. My memory isn't what it used to be."

My patience was wearing thin. I was always taught to respect my elders, but this lady was seriously cutting into my precious bedtime. "Well, I don't know what else to do here..."

"If it's not too much trouble... could I possibly get a ride home?"

I couldn't tell if it was the cold or if it was tremors, but her body was shaking back and forth like a tree in the wind. She continued,

"I know it's asking a lot… but I would be so very grateful. I'm close by, no more than ten minutes from here. I promise."

It was my turn to sigh. I cursed Mikael under my breath as I tapped my head against the steering wheel. "Okay. So what is your address?"

Her eyes perked up. "Oh, bless you, dear!"

She slowly told me her address as I typed it into my navigation app.

Four-minute drive.

"Okay, buckle up. Let's go."

She smiled warmly and patted me on the shoulder. "Thank you, dear. You are such an angel."

My stomach growled.

I started the engine and pulled away. I nearly turned out of the parking lot before I remembered.

The pizza.

The triple cheese that I had cooked—after hours and off the books—flashed back into my memory. The one sitting on the counter, the one I planned to gorge on while watching a movie before bed.

Giovanni's menacing snarl surfaced, the vein pulsating in his neck:

Your ass or your paycheck.

I knew if I left the pizza Giovanni would have questions. That was a problem I just couldn't ignore. I valued *both* my ass and my paycheck.

I circled back around, parking the car in front of the pizza shop. "Sorry," I apologized to the lady. "I have to run in for a moment. It will only take a sec."

I sprinted toward the front door. Glancing back, the lady gave me a nervous, wide-eyed stare. "I'll be quick. Just sit tight."

The box was still sitting on the counter. I opened it up and felt the layer of cheese. Cold. Ice cold. Normally, I would have just grabbed it and headed home. Pizza was great in any condition. But tonight, for some reason, I was craving it piping hot. The lady had waited this long, what was another couple of minutes? So I decided to quickly throw it back into the oven.

Ten minutes to bake. It's free if it's late.

The stupid slogan was burned into my memory.

Once the cheese was sizzling, I tossed the pizza back in the box, locked the door, and ran back to the vehicle.

When I returned, the car was empty. The lady was gone.

❖

Jimmy went into the closet and grabbed a plastic container of something.

"What is that, Jimmy?"

"It's feeding time," he stated, an evil grin spreading across his face.

The flies were buzzing around in a manic state, bouncing off the walls of the container.

"All you do is open the top, slowly," he instructed. Jimmy opened the top of the tank, then twisted the top of the container open, carefully aiming the opening toward the glass wall. They flew out like bats out of hell. He slid the roof of the tank shut before they could escape.

Many of the flies landed on what they thought were pretty fuchsia pedals. A lightning swipe of the pincers crumpled their unsuspecting bodies. The stem of the flower shook from side to side, as bit by bit was consumed. We watched for a while, in awe, as the flies began to slowly disappear.

"This is the coolest thing ever, Jimmy."

"I know, ain't it?" he said, pausing to take it all in. "Please don't tell anyone I did this. My Mom said I have to wait. The animals are my brother's, but they will be my responsibility when he leaves for college." He grinned. "Just one more year and they'll be mine."

We watched as the bug ate another and another.

"You think it will get them all?" I asked.

"No," he said, pointing to the corner of the tank. "These flies only live for a day or so. Most get eaten up. But some just whiz around the corner of the tank all day and die."

"Smart, I guess."

"Or dumb. Or lucky, I guess. Just depends on how you look at it." He moved closer to the tank. "Look at the real flower petals. The fuchsia is a lot deeper than the color of the bug's back. The texture is different, too. Come—look closely."

I pressed my face against the glass as another tiny, hairy head was ripped from its thorax.

"Wow. You're right! They are different."

He nodded, getting to his feet. "Yeah, it's subtle. Most people don't even notice it. But maybe some of them can tell." He opened the door. "Maybe it's a subconscious thing or something."

"Hey," I interjected, "earlier you said you needed me to do something?" He gently closed the door to his brother's bedroom, jiggling the knob to ensure it remained locked.

"Oh, yeah. I totally forgot. Don't worry about it."

"No," I insisted. "Tell me what it is, and I'll do it."

At the top of the stairs, we could hear the chaos. War had been waged once again.

Jimmy stopped awkwardly and seemed to shrivel up in shame. "I... I just wanted you to promise to always be my friend."

I placed my hand on Jimmy's shoulder, and before we entered the battlefield, I told him yes.

◈

I closed the newspaper in quiet reflection, still thinking about Jimmy.

All of the good times, all of the bad.

I drained the last sip of coffee, the sunshine filling up the room. The last precious moments of quiet before the family awoke.

No matter how hard you try to forget, the brain has a funny way of making you remember. All it takes is a trigger, and before you know it, that dusty memory begins to resurface. Whether you like it or not, it's always there.

Jimmy did get his chance to care for the animals. For a couple of months, we handled them with care: cleaning the tanks, preparing the meals, and making sure the salt levels were adequate. I got to see the flower bug up close, who we eventually named Richie. I even got to handle him a couple of times, later learning that he was actually an Orchid Mantis.

It was an amazing time, full of wonder.

Until Jimmy's brother came home from university for Thanksgiving, unannounced. He figured out that Jimmy had made a discovery. The boy had snooped around where he shouldn't have and found his brother's panty stash. The underwear he had uncovered from the closet was white and purple lace, and they were covered in crusty blood. I know this because he had promised me to secrecy. Jimmy had tried to place the item back the way it was, but he still found out.

They found Jimmy floating in the ravine. His face had been bashed in. His brother never looked the type; he was always very friendly and considerate to me. But apparently, he had been pounding his little brother's head in for years, only this time he made it count.

That was the worst memory of Jimmy. Not one I cared to recall.

But this wasn't the memory that clawed at me, still.

The headline read: *"Daring Escape for Good Samaritan"*. A teenager had offered a ride to someone she thought was in need and claimed to have escaped a near abduction.

I read it again... my stomach clenched.

The teen said she had sensed *something* from the beginning. Something was off that she couldn't explain. The encounter was awkward. The passenger seemed nervous, she recalled, swaying back and forth. And it was the glimpse of duct tape in the backpack that finally forced her hand.

By some dumb (or smart) stroke of luck, she had decided to leave. Out of nowhere, my daughter and son barreled down the hall. They surprised me, hanging off my back, as I smiled and ruffled their hair. My wife groggily trudged in afterwards, heading straight to the coffee maker.

It was the start of another beautiful, hectic day.

After breakfast, I decided to take a drive. I drove down O'Harra, south on Upton road, and made a left on 52nd street. The old Metropolitan Plaza was the same, all the businesses were just as I remembered. There was Giovanni's Pie's, Carlton's Electronics, Cece's Coffee and Coin & Go Laundry.

Only this time, I looked closer. I drove slowly through the lot.

I was looking for an answer to a question that had been gnawing at me all these years.

My hands quivered on the wheel as I made three laps around the plaza. I had confirmed my biggest fear, something I felt certain of, but never wanted to believe.

There was no pharmacy in the plaza.

I sat in my car, a sweaty mess. Thinking about Jimmy.

That night he had watched over me. And I've been looking closer, ever since.

THE VULTURES

My daughter was all grown up. It was a challenging thing for me to accept. I know it's how life is supposed to work, but that doesn't make it any easier.

My hands were stuffed inside my pockets as I wandered around the foyer. Kendra used to crawl up and down these halls, fumbling around in her diapers. I used to hear her gibberish all the way up the stairs. Now she was standing in the foyer, all her possessions sealed in cardboard boxes.

Off to College. Ohio State. She was going to be a Buck-Eye just like her father.

"Did you make sure you have everything?" Miranda asked, tears welling up in her eyes.

"Yes, Mom," she smiled. "Triple-checked, just like you asked."

"Parker checked the fluid levels?" I asked.

"Yes, Dad."

We stood in silence, all stalling tactics thoroughly exhausted. The only words left were goodbye.

Tears flooded from Miranda's eyes, a stream of black mascara steadily running down both cheeks as she wished our daughter good luck.

I bit down hard on my cheek as I bear-hugged Kendra. Once she broke free from my embrace, I quickly wiped away the salty trickle from my eyes.

"Don't get so worked up guys," Kendra said. "I'll be back in the summer."

"And for Christmas?" Miranda enquired.

"And Christmas."

"Reading break too," I reminded her.

She flashed another smile as she opened the door. "It's a really long drive, Dad. But we'll see."

Kendra grabbed the last of the cardboard boxes and promised to text us once she arrived.

One last kiss goodbye, one last I love you. And just like that, our grown-up daughter was gone.

✦

As far as I was concerned, no one would ever be good enough for my daughter. Plenty of people heaped praise over how exceptionally gorgeous she was. She was tall and slender—just like her father—but her most striking features were inherited from her mother: amber eyes that blazed with tenacity, soft skin, and rolling cinnamon locks. Her selflessness—an endless capacity for love that seemed to beam out of her—I had no idea where she got that from, but I was damn grateful that it was a part of who she was.

As she got older, I tried my best to lay down the law. No partying. No boyfriends. I ruled with an iron fist in order to protect her. But really, it was out of fear. I knew how teenage boys could be (and that terrified me greatly), but I soon realized that I was fighting a losing battle. As time went on, she retreated more and more into her phone, opting to text and giggle in her room over spending time with her family. I would find paintings and sketches of her scattered atop her dresser. The boys were swooping in, despite my best efforts. By the time she was a teenager all of her friends had boyfriends, which meant she must have coveted one too. I began to ease off, relinquish control, and trust Kendra to make her own decisions. That's all parenting was: pivoting. I figured the devil you knew was better than the one you didn't, so I began to relax the house rules.

And lo and behold, there came Parker.

When she first introduced me to her boyfriend, I was reluctant to accept him into our family. He was a nice enough kid, but again, my daughter deserved the world. I saw too much uncertainty in his character; he lacked confidence and direction. He was young, they were young. And looking back, at his age, I maybe saw too much of myself.

But the kid started to grow on me after a while. He stuck around the house like mold between grout. No matter how hard you tried, you couldn't scrub the kid away.

He didn't have a "manly man" bravado, he was more of a sensitive, artsy type. He never had much of a father, at least not one that paid him much attention. I taught him a lot: mostly simple handyman jobs like fixing his brakes, changing tires, and repairing things around the house. In exchange, he treated my daughter like gold. It was an unspoken arrangement, but both sides understood the terms.

I was incredibly proud of the progress he had made over the years. He decided to pick himself up by the bootstraps in his final year of high school. He hunkered down like I knew he could, studying and sacrificing to boost his grades up enough to give himself a chance.

I was just as ecstatic for him when I found out he got accepted into college. Ohio State, of all places.

No one would ever be good enough for Kendra, but that kid, Parker, was as close as they came.

Miranda and I looked forward to the occasional phone call on the weekend. They were mostly updates about the weather and therapy sessions about the difficulty of her course load, but Kendra's bubbly personality radiated through the speaker and always seemed to lift our spirits. She always checked in, even if there was nothing to talk about.

In her absence, I was left with a void that I didn't know how to fill. I found myself spending more time in the garage, tinkering with projects to keep me busy. Oftentimes, I found myself drifting into her old bedroom.

The posters from the pop bands she used to love were still plastered to her mauve painted walls as if she never left.

I would catch Miranda aimlessly drifting into Kendra's room too. On occasion, we would meet on her bed talking until the day faded into night. Days drifted into months, months drifted into semesters. We filled our voids as best we could.

There were two weeks left before Christmas and Kendra was coming home. Miranda had overdone it this year with decorations, in anticipation of the big day. One afternoon, I was changing the oil in Miranda's Oldsmobile when I received a phone call from Parker. It had been a long time since we'd spoken, so I eagerly picked up the call.

"Hello?"

"Hi, Mr. Sterling. Sorry to bother you. I know I shouldn't be calling you anymore. But I just didn't know who else to turn to." His usual upbeat tone sounded frantic and shaken.

"Oh nonsense, Parker. What's wrong?"

He choked up. "I don't even know where to start."

Through quick-breathed words and abrupt silences, Parker detailed the bout of bad luck that he had been having. The windows in his car had been smashed a couple of months ago. Last week the apartment he was renting had been broken into. The place had been ransacked, with most of his belongings being stolen or destroyed.

"Jesus, Parker," I sighed. "Kendra never mentioned any of this."

"We didn't want to scare you and all," he said. "I've been picking up some shifts in between classes at the bar to try to cover the damages."

"If you don't tell us, how can we help?"

"Well, it's not your problem anymore," he paused. "I'm just... I don't know. Scared. Thanks for letting me vent."

I opened up the bank app on my phone. "I'll send over some money to Kendra tonight. I just don't want to bother her while she's in class."

There was silence from the other end of the line.

"Don't worry about paying me back. Just change your locks while you guys look for another apartment and try to be more alert next time. You know, park in well-lit places in plain sight. That sort of thing."

More silence. I thought maybe the call had dropped.

"Parker?"

He whispered something, almost to himself, "She really didn't tell you?"

"Tell me what?"

A deep breath from the other line.

"Kendra and I broke up."

The words rattled inside my head. "I... I had no idea, Parker. I'm so sorry to hear that."

"It's okay, Mr. Sterling," he said with a bit of feigned optimism. "I'm going to win her back."

Before Parker hung up, he added: "Also, just so you are aware... Kendra isn't taking any classes at the moment. She dropped out this semester."

The two weeks crawled by at a sluggardly pace. Every day that passed I tussled with a gnawing urge to pick up the phone and confront my daughter. It was less anger that I felt and more of a stabbing disappointment.

"We don't know the whole story," Miranda said. "Before you jump to conclusions, let's give her a chance to explain."

The contents of Kendra's closet were laid out on the carpet, carefully extracted like evidence from a crime scene. Miranda was busy rummaging through her drawers, while I inspected the items laid out on the floor. It was an invasion of privacy, no doubt about it, and something Miranda and I had promised ourselves we'd never do. But Kendra left us no other option. If what Parker said was true, her tuition fund had been drained and God knows what she was doing with the monthly stipend we had been sending her.

The document that started it all seemed to lay there with a glowing aura. I had read through the letter multiple times, I could nearly recite it from memory.

Dear Kendra Sterling:

Congratulations! You have been offered admission to the Ohio State University, Columbus campus.

The letter was signed by the Director of Admission. The evidence was clear, she had been accepted. So why was she not in class?

"That's the last of it," Miranda said. "She'll be here soon. We have to hurry."

My eyes widened as I looked at the clock. "Damn it, Miranda! We should have done this days ago like I'd asked!"

Kendra was due any minute, and her room was in utter disarray like a tornado had blown through.

"Oh shut up, James. You're lucky I'm even a part of this to begin with. I wanted to talk, not excavate our daughter's bedroom."

We continued to argue as we rummaged through the pile of items. There were stacks of printed letters (mostly handwritten) and articles of jewelry (some inscribed with Kendra's initials) that we had never seen before. It would take days to go through the mountain of items.

I narrowed in on a peculiar drawing at the top of the pile. This one was not like the others dedicated to my daughter. The sketch was a figure of someone falling, flailing in the air. The darkness swallowed this figure up: around this dark vortex were words that were scratched in with such pressure that the paper nearly ripped through. Words like "MONSTER" and "EVIL". At the top of the paper was a thin yellow beacon of light.

My skin crawled as I reached for the letter that accompanied the sketch.

Dear Kendra,

I hope this gets to you, my princess.

I am always thinking of you in this endless darkness.

You are the light that keeps me going when...

The doorbell rang.

... there is nothing else. When no one else believes, you are the light that shines true.

The letter went on and on like this for pages. I cringed at every word.

Skipping to the last page:

I wish every day that circumstances were different. I wish I could get you everything you ever needed. Everything you ever longed for.

I don't deserve anything, but it seems God has shown pity on my soul. He has given me a gift in you that I will forever cherish.

Love,

K. Bowen

The doorbell rang again, accompanied by a steady flurry of knocks.

The last name had stopped me dead in my tracks. It sounded so familiar. I grasped for the connection in my brain, flipping through a rolodex in my mind: faces and names of snot-nosed kids that had been around the house before, they flickered in my memory. As quickly as they entered, they were tossed away. The third ring snapped me out of my thoughts.

"Miranda!"

Her head was down too, deeply enthralled by another letter she was reading.

She looked up, clearly startled. Her face was lily-white as she mumbled something to herself, the words still transferring from the paper to her brain.

"Clean up as best you can. I'll go grab the door."

She nodded as I headed down the hall.

Her face was just as I remembered. Her auburn eyes were fierce and glowing, the crease lines from her smile flowing into the tiny crevices of her dimples. She looked happy. She was a lot of things that night, but the most important thing was that she was here. After a warm embrace and teary eyes, we moseyed into the kitchen.

We gathered at the dinner table as Miranda made her rounds, plopping mashed potatoes onto our plates.

It was such a happy moment; I wanted to hold onto it forever. But I knew that I couldn't. We needed answers.

"So how did the midterms go?" I asked, a counterfeit smile across my face.

"They went okay," she smiled. "I know I nailed Psych 101. But the others... I'm not too sure."

My stomach tightened. The lie stung even more in person.

Miranda sat there with pursed lips, clearly disapproving of my deceitful approach. She stared, not at me, but through me, as if her mind was in another place.

"Well that's great, honey," I said flatly through gritted teeth. "I know it's been stressful, but I'm sure you did well. We are so incredibly proud of you."

"You guys worry too much," she replied, sawing through her roast beef and dipping the piece in a pool of gravy.

"We're your parents, that's our job," I said.

The temperature of the room was toasty warm, the fireplace blazing. The heat was amplified by the anger bubbling up inside of me as I watched Kendra effortlessly weave together her lies.

"So, where's Parker?" I asked.

Looking down at her plate, she spoke through a cheek full of mashed potato, "Oh, he couldn't make it. He picked up a bunch of shifts during the holidays, so he decided to stay in Columbus."

Miranda was trembling as she stared at the empty plate and cutlery set out for Parker. We knew he would be absent, but we played our part. "Well, that's a shame, dear," she said. "We were really looking forward to catching up with the both of you. His parents must be pretty upset, not being able to see him during the holidays and all."

"I think they'll understand. They—"

"Oh, cut the crap!" I finally shouted, my fist banging against the table. The abruptness stunned Kendra. Her shocked expression shifted between myself and Miranda.

"We know everything," Miranda jumped in.

"Know what?" she asked softly.

We offered nothing but our sullen expressions.

Her flimsy smile quickly withered into a frown. "He told you? I can't believe it..." she cried. "Do we really have to do this *now*?"

"Right now," Miranda pushed.

"Seriously, Mom?" she whined. "Parker thinks he knows everything, but he doesn't know a thing."

"Well, enlighten us then," I said. "Please."

Our food had grown cold, untouched, as we waited for our daughter's explanation.

"Things with Parker are complicated," she sighed, staring into her plate. "I wouldn't say things are over. We're just taking a little break."

Silence ensued as Miranda and I processed her words. While my anger simmered at an uncomfortable level, Miranda looked distraught. Her eyes were glazed over with a layer of moisture, her lips trembling.

"K... Kendra—" she stuttered, her voice trailing off into a fit of sobbing.

I shook my head. "I just don't understand the lies, Kendra." I refilled my glass with a generous pour of whiskey. In the reflection of the booze, I saw a tired old man. "What about the classes? Were you ever going to tell us?"

"I was. I was working up the courage. I'm sorry."

"Well, here's your opportunity!" I exclaimed. "Come clean about everything. Or you can kiss Columbus goodbye."

Kendra halted a moment before continuing. Her mouth wavered, opening then closing shut. Her words were seemingly stuck in her throat, as she chose them carefully. "I have a friend. He's misunderstood. He is such a talented artist and a wonderful soul. We've been communicating back and forth for years, well before I met Parker."

She swallowed, her eyes flashing in my direction. "Oh, you would love him, Dad, once you got to know him. He's funny and charming, just like you. He's the whole reason I wanted to go to Ohio." She took a long sip of water then continued, "I didn't think I'd ever get to see him. But this month it looks like everything could change."

I can't explain what it was about her combination of words, but for some reason, they triggered a connection in my brain. It finally clicked. The vault in my subconscious opened up, allowing access to memories of the person addressed in the letter. When I understood, my body froze.

"His name is Ken," she said. "Ken Bowen."

"Kendra..."

She nodded.

Miranda gasped, her head collapsing in her hands.

"See, I knew you would react like this," Kendra floundered, tears in her eyes. She grabbed her phone out of her purse and dialed, placing it on the table. "He's not what he's been made out to be. Don't be so quick to judge."

"Kendra, stop," I commanded, grasping for the phone. "What are you doing? Let's talk this through."

Her lightning quick reflexes snatched it away. She put the phone on speaker as it rang.

"You wanted the truth? Well here's the truth. Everything on the table."

There was our daughter: our prized possession, a spitting image of her mother and father. The sum of all of our sacrifices. Every word spilling out of her mouth tearing a hole through our hearts.

"It was wrong of me to keep these things from you. I didn't enroll this semester, it's true. But I needed time to get his affairs in order."

Miranda was consumed by despair, her hands covering her face. "Taking your money was wrong, I know that. I'm seriously so sorry. But I'm going to pay you back. Every penny. Once this hearing is over."

The speakerphone blared:

You are making a collect call to Ohio State Penitentiary.

I shuddered at the rows of black body bags that were recalled in my memory. The pools of blood, the shooting spree that Ken Bowen and his gang of baby-faced friends had orchestrated that dark December. The manhunt lasted months and spanned across multiple state lines. More seemingly anonymous bodies fell in their wake as they managed to elude authorities for months. A few of his riff-raff crew managed to escape, but Ken wasn't so lucky.

They were young, only kids back then. But so was I when the story first broke.

It had been years since I last heard his name. If I remembered correctly, his lawyers tried to argue insanity. The story had faded into oblivion. Shootings and massacres seemed to pile up over the years, replacing each other, one by one. All working together to keep the news cycle fresh. This was America, after all. There was always something new to be afraid of.

Kendra's auburn eyes stared into mine, our daughter that had all grown up.

"Give him a chance, Dad," she stammered. "I... I think I love him."

NANNY ELDA

It wasn't knocking. It was pounding. A banging, like thunder, rattled the patio door and echoed down the hall.

I glanced at my sister, Sofia, and my brother, Milo. We were huddled around Nanny's bedside, spooked by the intensity of the sound.

Boom. Boom. Boom.

The pounding persisted.

"Holy Christ. Let's not all get up at once," I muttered. I nodded to Sofia to stay with Nanny then tugged at my brother Milo's arm to come with me. He begrudgingly obliged, a wary look in his eyes.

We followed the banging, tip-toeing carefully down the hall.

Peering through the peephole, I saw a motley crew of characters on our porch. The light was dim, but I could still make out the silhouettes of Deputy Ronald, old man Gumble, our neighbor Mary Mack, and the Cowten twins.

Old man Gumble was the one crashing his fist against the door. His scowling face and liver-spotted hands kept pounding away like we owed him rent. The impact forced me to recoil from the peephole.

" Do... do we open it?" I asked.

Milo's face was drained of everything. Expression. Color. Courage. "Gee... I don't know. They look pissed." He paused, peeking through the_corner of the drawn blinds. "Were you and Sofia stealing candy from him again?

I nearly slapped him. "For God's sake, Milo. That was once... when we were little kids."

"Open up," Deputy Ronald barked. "We know you're in there. We need to speak to you, Elda."

I bit my nails as old man Gumble kept pounding away. For a seventy-year-old man, he sure could punch with conviction.

We were always taught to respect our elders, like most people from the town of Berkville. That's why this late-night visit was so jarring. They knew this was past Nanny's bedtime. They knew she needed her rest.

We were taught to respect our elders in this town, especially Nanny Elda. She was something of a town legend. Everyone had their stories. But her own, from her childhood, from a country far, far away from Berkville, those_stories were of survival. Real struggle, real poverty that my siblings and I would never understand. She used to joke that being poor in Canada was like winning the lottery. When she moved to Berkville, a single mother, she had nothing by western standards: just a thick accent and an immigrant's work ethic that never quit.

When mom and dad split and left town, we were all Nanny had. She was a single mother, again, trying to provide for three young children. She put up with a lot; we were often a bunch of rambunctious tornadoes. When we tore through the house, amidst all of the roughhousing and play fighting, we would often develop headaches that Nanny would help soothe with her famous remedy: an ice pack and some fatty fish soup, a recipe from her village.

She was there for everything. The teacher-parent conferences. The softball games. When my first boyfriend Andrew Cowten ditched me, she stayed by my side and got me all of the ice cream I could stomach. She was always there.

With the three of us, Nanny Elda had a really hectic schedule. She worked a couple of jobs to make ends meet. When we were younger, she would often bring us along with her to work. We used to love going to Mr. Culligan's Toy Shop, where she worked as a cashier in the evenings. It was impossible to get bored there: stacked on shelves as high as the ceiling were all of the action figures and Barbie dolls that a kid could ever dream of.

Mr. Culligan was a truly good man who brought so much joy to Berkville. He knew our situation and used to let Nanny sell some of her knit goods at the store and keep all of the profit. After his heart attack, Nanny helped manage the store and kept the doors open. When he eventually passed, the whole town was devastated. The day of the funeral was the first time I had ever seen her cry. Somber sobs for a man who left a gaping hole in the world. When the dust settled, we were shocked to find out that he had left the toy shop to Nanny Elda in his will.

Not to his kids. Not to his widow.

He must have seen something in Nanny: whether it was her persistent work ethic or her go-getter mentality. Or maybe he sympathized with our circumstance. Whatever it was, Nanny was ecstatic. But I believe this was the start of all of the stories. All of the rumors—the nasty activities that housewives partake in to pass the time. It never bothered Nanny; she was never one to care about other people's opinions. She continued to keep her nose to the grindstone and focused on building her business. She built relationships with suppliers and began to sell exclusive toys that couldn't be found in our province. She found ways to export her product overseas. The toy shop quickly expanded, and Nanny ran multiple shops in the city and in nearby satellite towns. She even diversified her portfolio, purchasing the Berkville hardware store and laundromat.

In this tumbleweed, forgotten, blip of a town, Nanny Elda stuck around. Her toy shop put Berkville on the map, people visited from far and wide. She completely transformed her life, from a struggling immigrant to one of the wealthiest business owners Berkville had ever known. And the profit trickled down to all of the nearby businesses and residents.

Clearly, none of that mattered tonight.

"Open up!" Mary Mack hollered.

I finally had had enough and unlatched the door. "What do you people want? Do you realize how late it is?"

"Oh, evening, Delilah," old man Gumble smirked, his face wrinkled like worn leather. "Took you mighty long to open up."

"What do you want?" I repeated.

The porch light shone with a murky apricot glow.

Sheriff Ronald, the volunteer sheriff, took a step forward and puffed out his chest. His tan uniform was faded along the seams, his body testing the limits of the fabric. A nickel star-shaped badge was pinned to this chest. The badge that nobody else wanted.

"Hi, Delilah. Sorry to bother you. Mary Mack said she saw your Grandma come home from the hospital. Is everything alright?"

In this town, we were taught to respect our elders. But apparently, not each other's privacy.

Milo popped his head into the doorway. "Go away, please. She's sleeping."

I added, "Please come back tomorrow after she's had some rest. We're all tired." It had been a tumultuous couple of days, and I just couldn't let them disturb Nanny.

"*Tired*?" the Cowten twins scoffed.

Sheriff Ronald put his hand on the door. Old man Gumble followed. "We will only be a couple of minutes," Sheriff Ronald assured us. "We just want to ask her a few questions."

They applied pressure. Milo and I planted our feet and strained, pushing the door closed with all our might. We heard the door creaking, crying, from the distress.

"Let go!" Milo huffed through clenched teeth.

The door swung open, catapulting back off the doorstop. We fell to the floor, as old man Gumble stepped over us and down the hall.

"Stop!" I bellowed.

Milo grabbed old man Gumble's bony calf and wrestled him to the floor. They struggled for a while before Gumble donkey kicked him in the face. I cried out for help, but the old man threatened to hit me too.

There were too many of them. And we were just kids.

The Cowten twins waltzed in, brandishing their previously concealed shovels. Matching shovels, likely purchased from the Berkville hardware store. Nanny Elda's hardware store. Rust and dirt flaked off the heads of the shovels as they dragged them across the hardwood.

Mary Mack, our beloved neighbor, the undercover spy, she surged over our helpless bodies, catching up to the search party.

"*Nanny Elda*?" she called out, in a taunting glee.

I lifted myself up off the floor and shuffled towards Milo. His thick mop of midnight-black was damp and warm in the front.

Warm with blood.

"Where are you hiding her, Delilah?" Old man Gumble yelled.

I charged down the hall, following the scraping of the shovels. The intruders weaved in and out of the rooms, disappearing and reappearing. When they realized the rooms were empty, they slammed the doors shut.

I caught up to Sheriff Ronald and yanked on his sleeve. "Get the hell out of our house. Now!"

He smacked me in the face with a swat that sent me backward. I hit the wall, the taste of blood in my mouth. The Cowten twins, with their shovels now tossed to the floor, held me down and kneeled on my shoulders. Their auburn pigtails swayed back and forth above my face.

One of them whispered softly into my ear, "I always thought Andrew was too good for you."

The group made their way to the last door down the hall—Nanny Elda's bedroom.

Sheriff Ronald turned the knob to no avail. "Nanny Elda, open up!" he urged. "We have some questions for you, my dear. If you cooperate, it won't take long."

Old man Gumble beat up on the door again with loud, empty thuds.

I pictured Sofia weeping next to Nanny's bedside. Shaking, not knowing what to do. The helplessness, the thought of my family left there unprotected, caused me to begin to erupt in a barrage of tears and shrieks.

The door wasn't budging, so Mary Mack threw her shoulder into the mix. "Andrew Cowten! Margy Gumble! Tell us what you did to them!" You could hear cracking as the side of the door began to splinter. "I heard you talking about them in your dirty language. Where are they? Where are you hiding them?"

Everyone had their stories. Now I knew how far this town would go to find answers.

A jarring snap, like a twig broken in half against your knee. The sound silenced Mary Mack for a moment. It sent old man Gumble to the floor in a crumpled, yelping heap. His eyes were stretched wide, his body stiff as a board. Sheriff Ronald froze. Mary Mack screamed.

Another crunch and one of the Cowten twins' neck's folded in half, the shattered bone leaving a lumpy bulge pushed up against the skin. Her head drooped, heavy, resting momentarily on her shoulder. Her pigtails fell, brushing against my face. Then she collapsed. Her sister shrieked.

The intruders evacuated the house, leaving behind the Cowten sister and old man Gumble sprawled out on the floor.

I stepped around his immobile body, his hysterical screaming making me cringe. It was largely incoherent, except for a few words:

"Lord Jesus, Help! I can't feel my legs!"

I knocked on what was left of the door. "Sofia! It's Delilah. They're gone now. It's safe."

There was no response, only faint beeping coming from the other side. I pulled the pieces of the caved-in wood apart, tossing away the remains of the door. I could see the back of Nanny's dresser pushed up against the entrance. I pushed a little, and it moved an inch. I pushed harder, and it moved a little more. Eventually, I could hear the pumping of the life support machine. When there was enough space to fit through, I ducked under the battered hole of splintered wood and maneuvered my way through the gap.

Sofia was sitting in the dark, laid back in a chair. She was whispering something and rocking back and forth, tears running down her unblemished face. Something was clutched close to her chest. I wrapped my arms around her and tried my best to soothe her.

"They're gone now, baby. They can't hurt us. Everything will be okay."

The room was dark, except for the blinking lights from the machine. I approached the beeping, leaning next to Nanny's bedside. Her body looked gaunt, the skeletal curves of her collarbone threatening to poke out of her skin. But her eyes were full of life. They were open—darting swiftly back at Sofia, then back at me.

Something pricked me. I grabbed the object. I could see something sharp was poking through the fabric. Flipping the object over and holding it up against the lights, I could make out the outline of a doll. Sewn-together burlap with reddish-brown strings hanging from the head. The stuffing popped out of the neck.

Sofia shook in the darkness, rocking back and forth in her chair.

⬡

Things went quiet for a while. The townspeople seemed to have left us alone to grieve. But I am terrified they will come back, much more prepared and larger in numbers. I don't know how we will hold them off next time; we might not be so lucky.

Nanny's health hasn't improved. She is conscious, her eyes are moving, but her body is still deteriorating. It's a miracle she's still here given the severity of the stroke. But I don't know how much longer we can keep her on life support.

I'm worried about Sofia now too. She's become distant, barely speaking to anyone at school. At least that's what her teachers say. She just wants to be left alone to play with her toys. We found a whole box of dolls tucked away in Nanny's closet.

That night of retribution, the ambulance arrived for Milo and old man Gumble. Milo was fine, they sent him back home to rest off his concussion, but Gumble's situation was far more serious. The paramedics said that the old man must have slipped and broken his back. His bones were fragile. All that commotion wasn't good for a man his age. As for the Cowten sister, they weren't quite sure what happened. The force fracture couldn't be explained.

All I know, is that this should be the last story about Nanny Elda.

DADDY WAS A DRIFTER

Noah's eighteenth birthday came and went with a flurry of emotions. There was jubilation for the festivities his mother had planned (she must have invited every person he'd ever known). Streamers were strung up along the walls, balloons hung from the ceiling, and there was even a slide show to sit through (which included some unflattering snapshots of his youth to the crowd's delight). Despite all of this, he couldn't shake a profound feeling of sadness. As everyone raised a glass for a toast—his first "official" beer—Noah's mind was elsewhere.

He was a "man" now. This fact weighed heavily on his psyche. He felt trepidation for his first year of college, being so far away from home. Fall was approaching quickly; he could feel that things were changing. But in this instance, this was not where his mind wandered. Amongst all of his closest friends and family, packed elbow to elbow to celebrate him, he couldn't help but fixate on the absence of one.

His thoughts were with his father.

Waves start as tiny ripples, so they say.

❖

The beating of a drum off in the distance—getting louder, getting closer. The feeling of vibrations running through my bones as I twitch and squirm.

A chant in an unfamiliar language:

"Osisifɔɔ"

"Osisifɔɔ"

"Osisifɔɔ"

Something covers my eyes, squeezing me from behind as I struggle to break free.

A momentary break from the curtain of darkness. A glimpse of cold steel placed upon my throat. A desperate shriek escapes my lungs.

The veins pulsate in my neck. I continue to fight.

Through the stretched-out fingertips, I see the group huddling around us. Thousands of motionless figures with emotionless gazes, looking on as the blood spurts out of my neck.

I fall to my knees.

❖

Noah awoke in a cold sweat, gasping for breath. His throat ached, his lungs burned. It felt as if he'd nearly drowned. At first, he chalked the dream up as just another nightmare. He was prone to having these "night terrors" from time to time. This time though, it was the regularity of the same dream that disturbed him. After the third night in a row where his throat was slit, each instance more real and sinister than the next, he began to question if there was something seriously wrong with his brain.

On the fourth morning, he found a crumpled-up note beside his nightstand. Rather than tossing it in the bin, he chose to unravel the scrap of paper. It read:

Bug.

Find ɔdɔ in the attic.
Burn this note.
Love,
Dad

It was written in an awful chicken scratch that was barely legible.

Goosebumps emerged on his neck as he re-read the note.

Bug.

He hadn't been called that since he was a little boy.

Love, Dad.

His insomnia was playing tricks on him; it was the only explanation. He stared at the ceiling, thinking, as raindrops pattered against his bedroom window. The morning chill signified that the last days of summer were all but over.

❖

Noah had mixed feelings about his father. He had split from the family when Noah was young. All that was left to cling to were fuzzy memories: a school trip here, a camping trip there. The three of them together. Happy. Or so he thought. He was beginning to recognize that humans were complicated beasts, and relationships were complicated things. What did he really understand about the inner workings of his parent's relationship? At that age, the reality was that he knew nothing. For someone he barely knew, his father still seemed to occupy a frustratingly large section of his brain.

Sometimes he would catch his mother looking at old photographs. Small albums, tucked away. He caught her wet-eyed on most occasions, flipping through the pages, recounting old memories of the past. In these moments, he loathed his father. He felt he was a selfish excuse for a man.

Then there were moments where he missed him dearly. He yearned for his direction, his hearty laughter, his playful demeanor.

Most of all, he wondered if his father would have been proud of who he became.

When his dad left, the family teetered on the brink of destruction. They bounced around a myriad of sleazy motels and one-bedroom apartments. For a while, Noah and his mother slept on the couches of various friends and distant relatives: aunties and uncles they seldom knew. Anyone who would take them in, they graciously accepted their offers. His mother juggled two jobs to stay afloat. She was resilient in her efforts, but it always felt like they were capsizing.

One day a stubby man walked into the restaurant where his mother was working. Noah started to slowly see him around more often, wherever their current dwelling was that week. Then one morning his mother packed their bags. They moved to Frank's place and never left again. Noah's mother and Frank eventually got married. They had two kids of their own and everyone blended into one brand-new family.

Noah's stepfather, Frank, couldn't have been a better person. He transformed their lives, forever. They were a middle-class family now with a home to call their own and a dog to chase around their yard. What more could a person ask for?

But to Noah, he would never be his father.

With these mixed emotions, he grabbed the note and scurried to the attic. He pulled down the ladder and climbed. A sprinkling of dust welcomed his presence; the cloud entered his throat and forced up a cough. As he poked his head up, a dim ray of light shone through a tiny crack in the siding. It was dark; he could barely make out the cobwebs dangling from the rafters. There was a layer of soot coating the room like a fresh snowfall in winter. He took a deep breath and turned on the flashlight on his phone. His nerves were on edge as he pulled himself upward, crouching as he cautiously made his way through this new environment. He half expected a ghost or some sort of presence to lunge at him, but there was no such occurrence. He was alone with a couple of spiders, drywall dust, and a row of boxes stacked in the corner of the room.

He dropped the note and started rummaging through the first stack like a madman. There were forgotten items he'd never seen before: antiques that looked like they would break if you stared at them too intensely. He ruffled through the items and made a pile on the floor: old trinkets, silverware, costume jewelry pieces. There was nothing out of the ordinary and nothing that related to the note.

Hours went by with no success. Noah stared across the dusty room at the last weathered box. There was a rip on the side with the edge of a photograph poking out. Noah pulled on it to discover it was a photo of his Mom and Dad. They were young and dressed in cocktail attire. *Bingo*, he thought, as he dug through the contents.

It was strange seeing photos of his parents before he was born. Their faces were the same, but the scenes that were captured were completely foreign to him. There were stories in these photos, likely never to be told.

The first thing he noticed was that their lifestyle before him looked drastically different. Half the photos were from different parts of the world; some places Noah didn't even recognize: Mom and Dad climbing through the Himalayas, posing together at the Great Wall, safari snapshots taken in the back of a jeep somewhere in Africa. Photos of vast deserts and lush jungles. It looked like his parents were part of a National Geographic documentary. His mind wandered between fascination and anger. Despite his pleas to see the world, the two of them had never left the city.

In the corner of the cardboard box, he found what he was looking for. There was a sealed wooden box the size of his palm. It was labeled "ɔdɔ" in ugly handwriting.

"Noah?"

His mother's face poked up from the entry point.

"What are you—" her eyes widened as she saw the slew of scattered photos.

"Noah…"

"Mom, what is this?" He threw his hands up in frustration. "You and Dad went to China? With no mention of this, ever?" He frowned, turning away. " You've been literally everywhere."

He was sick of being lied to, sick of being treated like a child

Her eyes flared with a fury that Noah had never witnessed before. "Put those back!" She hoisted herself up and charged at him, nearly hitting her head against one of the wooden beams. "Go downstairs. Now!" she commanded, the floorboards creaking with every menacing step. "The snooping around stops here." She dropped to her knees and clawed at the photos, chucking them with haste back into the box.

"I just want to know about him. That's all I've ever wanted."

"Oh you do, do you?" she barked back, tears streaming down her face. "Fine. Where do I start?"

Noah took a step back. Something was wrong. His mother's face did not look normal, it looked twisted in agony. He immediately regretted prodding for information. He backed away, tucking the small box beneath his waistband, concealing it under his shirt.

"Keetan was a low-life. A good-for-nothing drifter. All he cared about was seeing the world and checking a country off his bucket list. When I became pregnant, I thought things would change. I thought he would man up and provide for his family. And for a while, he did. Things were looking good. Then, I don't know what to say. One day he was gone. No mention or warning, no kiss goodbye." She winced. "That was your father, Noah."

Noah's heart sank with guilt. "I'm sorry, Mom…"

"Well, now you know," she said. Her years of struggle were evident, even in the dim light. The wrinkles carved by grief never went away.

They sat in silence for a while as she packed up the things. Before she left, she kissed Noah on the forehead. "Forget him, dear," she said, apologetically. "You are all the adventure I ever needed."

With a queasy feeling in his stomach, Noah followed his mother out of the attic. They both carried out their box of secrets: one weathered, one sealed.

That was the last time he saw those photos.

Noah waited patiently until dinner was over before escaping to his room. He pulled the box out from under his bed and broke the seal with a pair of scissors. Inside was the tiny skull of an animal with gaping orbital bones. Within the eyeholes were incense and another crumpled-up note. It read:

Bug,
In the skull:
Burn the incense.
Light the candle at midnight.
Bring a mirror.
Burn this note.
Love,
Dad

Another message shrouded in mystery. Noah's heart thrashed in his chest as he laid eyes on the same messy handwriting again. Most things were better left in the past; he did agree with his mother, but his curiosity would never let him walk away from this.

Stuffing the contents under his bed, his mind traveled across the world to the places his mother and father had been that he would never see for himself.

The clock struck midnight. Noah lit a match. The incense smelled like hints of wood and turmeric. He dipped the note into the flame, watching it burn into ash. He waited patiently behind the faint glow of the candle, staring back at the stressed-out reflection of himself in the mirror. Five minutes went by in the darkness. Ten minutes... and nothing. Then a swift whoosh of air extinguished the flame. Noah froze in terror, his vision blinded by the night. Then came another rapid gust of wind, and the flame came back to life. His father's face was in the mirror.

"Bug!" The man's smile curved from ear to ear. "You don't know how good it is to see you." His face looked sunken like he hadn't eaten in days.

Noah jolted backward. "*Dad*? is that really you?"

"It's really me, Noah. God, look at you, kid. All grown up." He didn't think his father's grin could get any larger, but it somehow stretched further. His eyes were glistening. "My boy's a man."

Noah's body was shaking. Almost vibrating. In a terrified haste, he lunged to blow out the candle.

"Noah?" his dad called.

"What the hell is this?"

"I know this is crazy... but I swear it's me."

He hesitated to ask the question, but knew it must be asked: "Are... are you a ghost?"

"I'm not, Noah. I'm still alive." He paused to wipe away some rogue tears that managed to escape. "I wanted to be around. If you only knew... I honestly did. I love you and your mother with all my heart."

"So why did you leave us like that? With nothing..."

"I'm sorry. It wasn't what I wanted. It never was what I wanted." This statement left Noah utterly confused. He sat there in silence.

"I need you to listen, son. What I'm about to say sounds utterly insane. It's before your time, I don't expect you to understand. But I promise you, every word is true. And there's not much time, we need to hurry."

Noah was certain now that he had gone mad. But he decided to indulge this reflection in the mirror that claimed to be his father. "What are you talking about? I don't understand."

"Listen—your mother and I traveled to Ghana before you were born. She got sick when we were there, terribly sick." He continued, "She was delirious. She was supposed to die from Malaria on that trip. An indigenous woman brought us to a shaman in a nearby village who helped revive her."

"What are you saying?"

"Please just listen. That came at a cost. I've been living on the run ever since. The shaman—he showed me how to cover my tracks, how to shift in and out of different planes of... of existence." He paused, noting the absurdity of his words. "You have to believe me! I managed to trick them for a while, managed to shelter you guys from it all. But I fear that... maybe... something is wrong. This is why I'm reaching out. On a suspicion, I guess. An inkling. I can feel something... something aching in my chest."

"Dad... you're scaring me."

"Noah, tell me. Tell me, please: have you seen anything in your dreams? Anything out of the ordinary."

Noah swallowed. "Something has been killing me for three nights straight."

"*Three nights*?" his father's eyes were large saucers.

Noah nodded. A look of devastation spread across his father's face. "Listen: you and your mother need to stay awake. Do you hear me? Go and wake her, immediately."

The desperation in his voice made Noah panic. "Okay, I will. But what does this mean?"

"Give me some time to fix this. Maybe a couple of days will be enough to throw them off the trail. At the very least, maybe I can negotiate something further."

"Okay."

"I love you, son. Go and wake her. And wait for a message back from me."

"Sounds good, love you."

And just like that, the flame was extinguished. Darkness flooded the room.

Noah took a moment to gather his thoughts. He still didn't fully understand, but his father was adamant about one thing:

Go and wake Mom.

Noah bolted to her bedroom. He could hear wheezy snoring coming from beyond the door.

He entered the bedroom to see his mother standing near the wall. A machete was held to her throat. Frank was sleeping peacefully, snoring on his side of the bed. Out like a light.

A tribesman with white face paint had one hand over her mouth, the other clutching the knife.

Noah tried to scream, but something stifled the sound. It was a familiar feeling—cold steel and a warm palm. The blade held up against his neck knicked his adam's apple. He felt a sharp sting as his breath ran shallow and weak.

There was silence as blood trickled down his neck. At his feet, something rolled towards him from under the bed. It was the crumpled-up note from the attic, the one he forgot to burn. The blood dripped onto the balled-up paper as the tribesman kicked it away.

"Osisifɔ."

"Osisifɔ."

"Osisifɔ."

The rest of the tribe's people emerged from the shadows, as the ripples turned into waves and the past finally met the present.

The tribesman crawled out from under the bed like spiders, their eyes eager to watch the fate of Noah and his mother.

"Osisifɔ."

"Osisifɔ."

"Osisifɔ."

The chanting filled the room. Every inch of carpet was now covered by a native savage. Their bone necklaces seemed to glow in the darkness.

Despite the noise, Frank slept, unaware of the present danger. Sheltered from the terror.

Suddenly, a pounding came from the wall. Not the wall—it was coming from the full-length mirror mounted to the wall. Noah's father had appeared, he was banging his fists against the other side of the mirror. There was a feral look in his eyes, his skinny arms swinging back and forth with ferocity. There was a crunch. The chanting stopped. The tribe suddenly turned their attention to the mirror. They tried to pry it from the wall as Noah's father's fists pumped back and forth like two pistons. It shattered just as it was removed, the shards of glass raining to the floor. It was just enough to stir Frank from his slumber.

"Noah?" his groggy voice called out in the darkness.

The tribe had disappeared. There was only Noah left, standing in the middle of the room and bleeding from his neck, and his mother, curled up on the floor.

"Rita?" Frank called out. He switched on a light. "Is everything okay?"

Mom looked lost. She mumbled something to herself before she caught her breath. "I... I'm fine. Just a bad dream. That's all."

"Jesus, Noah!" Frank shouted. He jumped out of bed and headed for the washroom. "Let me get you a band-aid. What the hell happened?"

Noah picked up one of the pieces of broken glass. He stared into the jagged shard and sighed. There was no last glimpse. Just the reflection of an exhausted, young man.

"Oh, nothing," he hollered back. "I knocked over the mirror, that's all."

The chant was still ringing in his ears, the fear still pulsating through his body. He managed to walk over to his mother and picked her up off the floor. He squeezed her tight in a close embrace.

In her ear, he whispered:

"Mom, we need to talk."

She began to cry as Frank stumbled in with the box of bandaids.

"It's Dad."

"It's Dad."

FIREWORKS

"Mommy, look!"

The sparks in the distance were like lightning. They lit up the desolate sky in momentary flashes—splashes of color on an otherwise void, starless canvas. Suzie held Callum's hand, leading him along the dirt road. They walked quickly, the wheels of his little suitcase clacking against the dirt.

"The fireworks are pretty tonight!" Callum exclaimed as a blaze of red and yellow exploded in a sparkly smear. They stopped to admire the display for a moment before the darkness engulfed the sky once again.

"*Shhh*," Suzie urged, putting a finger to her lips. She held him close for another moment before whispering, "They sure are beautiful, honey."

"Are we almost there?" the boy huffed. He had been battling with one of the wheels the whole journey, it wobbled and spun erratically, often opting to turn in random directions regardless of the momentum. She hated that damn suitcase. It was Gabe who had always promised to fix it. She was forbidden from purchasing a new one, and now look at where they were.

Suzie knew she was asking a lot from her five year old son. For them to have been so cautious for so long, it seemed insane to be doing what they were doing now. She imagined the poor boy's throbbing feet: blisters bubbling up from the hours of walking and the friction caused by his snug sneakers with the worn-out soles. Just the thought of it all made her cringe.

This may be our only chance, she told herself. They stopped at a chain-link fence. Suzie dug inside her pocket and pulled out the crinkled map. She took a quick scan of the directions. They were heading north toward the fireworks, which seemed odd to Suzie. But the instructions Gabe had left them were surprisingly neat and straightforward, which was very unlike her husband. She was used to chicken scratch drawings on the back of sticky notes (if he even remembered to write any and all). From the curvature of the letters to the very stroke marks on the map, everything was properly spaced, straight, and legible. Precise. Almost as if it were a document that had been typed. Suzie guessed it spoke to the predicament they were in, Gabe needed them to find their way.

According to the map, they needed to pass through the barrier in order to get to the freeway. Both the height of the fence and the barbed wire seemed a daunting task for the mother and son. Suzie surveyed the fence line for any breaks in the coverage. The barrier seemed to go on forever.

"C'mon, sweetie." She pointed a couple of yards ahead. "This way," she urged, gently tugging on the boy's collar.

A year ago, the size of the gap would have been a problem for her. But in her current emaciated state, she slithered her body through the slit in the fence like a garden snake, with minimal snags to her clothing. Callum looked excited—*finally some action*—as he swiftly crawled through the break in the fence like a trained soldier. He giggled, making a hushed cheer as he made it to the other side. A smile spread across Suzie's face.

Now is the hard part, Suzie thought. It would be a long slog to their destination.

Down the embankment, the highway was straight as an arrow toward the horizon. The asphalt plain went on as far as the eye could see. Both lanes were filled with what once was gridlock traffic, the cars long since abandoned and covered in a fine layer of dust.

Suzie stopped once more to study the directions. It had become a nervous habit of hers.

Left or right?

She pondered for a moment. Her reliance on GPS had made her stupider over the years. It had been a long time since she needed to make note of landmarks. She spun the map around accordingly, reorienting herself.

They set off down the highway, walking along the shoulder lane past the row of cars. The occasional firework display illuminated the sky. Besides the light show, a tiny beacon from Suzie's headlamp was their guiding light.

According to her directions, they were to head straight for a long time. Impossible to get lost, but grueling, nonetheless. She was at least grateful for the terrain. The hike through the forest, while sheltered, had been hard on her knees.

"Mommy?"

"Yes, Callum?"

"What are those things?" he asked, pointing up to a set of billboards off the freeway. The figures stood in place of the advertisements for theme parks and divorce lawyers that had long since been torn down.

"Oh, honey. Those are scarecrows. Remember back at the farm?"

"Why are there so many?" the boy asked. He had to squint to make out their figure. They stood high above the lampposts and vehicles lining the streets.

"There are lots more birds and pests to ward off here." The answer seemed to satisfy his curious mind, but she knew she couldn't lie to him forever.

With every passing moment, she could feel the boy getting restless. Time was elusive these days, but her feet told her that they had been walking for hours. They had made real progress so far; he had been such a good boy, much better than she thought he'd ever be. But as much as she wanted to, they couldn't stop.

"You hungry, Callum?"

He shook his head. "My belly hurts," he complained. "My legs too, Mom. I'm tired."

Suzie kept walking, yanking her backpack off and flipping it to the front of her chest. She was now wearing it like a kangaroo pouch. She unzipped the front pocket and investigated the contents inside.

"We're nearly there. Just keep going, dear. You're doing great."

He grunted. "How much longer?"

Suzie's heart sank when she pawed through the contents of her bag. The cold air of the night hit her fingers as they poked through one of the corners. She thought the bag had felt light, but this confirmed her wildest fears. All that was left were the freeze-dried bags of food that were too big to sneak through the ripped seam, and those would require boiled water to consume, precious time that they could not spare.

"Almost there, Callum. Keep pushing."

Another lie. They were a couple of hours away, at least, and that's if they kept a steady pace. Her boy was fading though, his stride looked laborious, the silence between them seemingly lulling him to a slow trot.

They kept walking.

"Why don't you tell me again, sweetie? What's the first thing you'll do in Providence?" She tried the handles of the vehicles as they passed by, they all appeared to be jam-packed with belongings so high you couldn't see out the back window. Maybe they would stumble across something of value that hadn't already been pillaged. Maybe they would get lucky for a change. A girl could only hope.

She kept telling herself that it would be worth it. Gabe had never been wrong before.

"Honey?"

Suzie turned around to the sound of shattering glass. Callum had flipped around his flashlight and battered the window of a nearby car. She forgot about the glass breaker on the butt of the shaft. The moment knocked the wind right out of her lungs.

She ran to her son and pulled at his waist in a desperate fury. "Callum!"

He was halfway inside the backseat before she could reach him. His legs dangled in the air, shards littering the pavement. His right hand was reaching for something, his left gripping the flashlight. They wrestled for a moment before Suzie could get a firm grip. She yanked him out of the backseat, his shirt covered in a dusting of shards of glass, his hands bleeding with slivers of window.

"What did I tell you!" Suzie cried.

Callum was sobbing uncontrollably.

Her heart sank when she saw what he was holding. In his hand was a giraffe stuffy, identical to the one she had forced him to leave behind.

"I miss home," the boy mumbled through sniffles. His body sank into his mother's, her arms wrapped around him like a protective cocoon.

They both held each other in a steady release of tears. It couldn't have been longer than thirty seconds.

That's all it took, thirty seconds, for the fleet to arrive.

The buzzing of hundreds of tiny motors filled the air. They came searing through the sky like a cloud of killer bees. The sound intensified in the blackness; all that could be seen were the tiny yellow flashing lights. She watched the blinking orbs pass the strung-up bodies on the billboards, the skeletons nailed to the wooden frames with outstretched arms like decaying statues of Jesus.

The swarm of machines floated down to their targets.

Suzie knew it was over. She was tired. Tired of the hiding. Tired of the running.

She had seen the aerial assaults once before. They had sliced through the sky and caught the running targets from miles away. Many other times, she heard the carnage but opted to head for shelter to protect the boy from witnessing the attacks.

She held her son close, for the last time, amongst the rows of abandoned vehicles. Another explosion set off in the night sky, signs that the war was still waging on.

The first line of attack hovered down towards them.

"Callum?" she asked. "Tell Momma again, what's the first thing you want to do in Providence?"

With one final sob, the boy cried:

"Hug Dad."

MORE CHILLS FROM VELOX BOOKS

MORE CHILLS FROM VELOX BOOKS

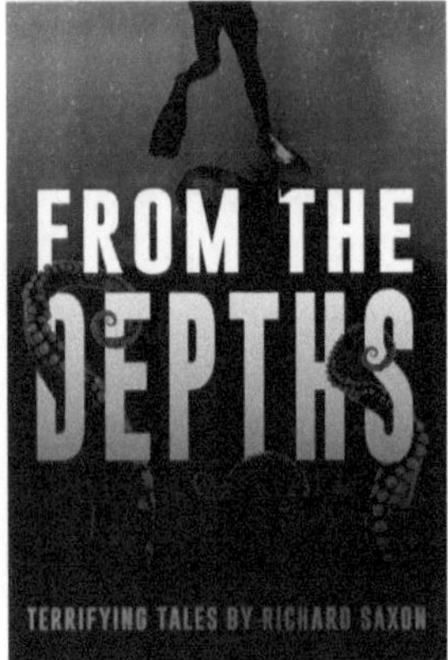

www.ingramcontent.com/pod-product-compliance
Lightning Source LLC
Chambersburg PA
CBHW061348310726
48974CB00001B/256